MW01139612

Other Books by Rae D. Magdon

Amendyr Series
The Second Sister - Book 1
Wolf's Eyes - Book 2

And with Michelle Magly

Dark Horizons

THE WITCH'S DAUGHTER

BY

RAE D. MAGDON

Desert Palm Press

The Witch's Daughter

Amendyr Series - Book 3

By Rae D. Magdon

©2015 Rae D. Magdon

ISBN: 9781508596950

All rights reserved. No part of this book may be reproduced in any form other than that which it was purchased and without the express permission of the author or publisher. Please note that piracy of copyrighted materials violate the author's right and is illegal.

This e-book is licensed for your personal enjoyment only. This e-book may not be re-sold or given away to other people. If you would like to share this book with another person, please purchase an additional copy for each recipient. If you're reading this book and did not purchase it, or it was not purchased for your use only, purchase your own copy. Thank you for respecting the hard work of this author.

This is a work of fiction. Names, characters, places, and incidents are the product of the author's imagination or used fictitiously and any resemblance to actual persons, living or dead, businesses, companies, events, or locales is entirely coincidental.

For permission requests, write to the publisher, addressed "Attention: Permissions Coordinator," at the address below.

Desert Palm Press
1961 Main Street, Suite 220
Watsonville, California 95076
www.desertpalmpress.com

Editor: Kellie Doherty (http://editreviseperfect.weebly.com/)

Cover Design: Rachel George (http://www.rachelgeorgeillustration.com/)

Printed in the United States of America
First Edition April 2015

Acknowledgement

To T, for everything, and for being my everything.

And to Lee and Kelly, who nurtured this work into its full potential.

THE WITCH'S DAUGHTER

PART ONE

Taken from the verbal accounts of Ailynn Gothel, Recorded and summarized by Lady Eleanor Kingsclere, née Sandleford

CHAPTER ONE

MY MOTHER TREASURED PRETTY things. When I was very young, she often took me into the treasure rooms to show me all of the beautiful objects she had collected. She liked to point out her favorites, and sometimes, if she was in a good mood, she told me how she had acquired them. She let me explore them, too, allowing me to run my fingertips over the gold chains, the elegant satin gowns, and the finely woven tapestries.

Mother never allowed any of our visitors to see the treasures. She did not like people, but they were the easiest way to expand her collection, and so she tolerated them. Sometimes. Whenever someone came to trade a new bauble for a magic spell, curse, or healing draught, she would give it to me, and I would take it through the front room and into the kitchen. There was a small wooden door beside the fireplace, and if you asked politely, it would take you to the treasure room. If the door was cranky, or if a stranger lingered in the house, it would simply lead out into the forest.

Despite the stories the villagers told, my mother was not a gruesome hag. She was incredibly beautiful, with skin so fair it could almost be called translucent and thick brown hair that tumbled over her shoulders in wild curls. I did not grow up to be quite so fair, but I resembled her much more than I would have liked. I was also cursed with my mother's magpie-like tendencies, but unlike her, I only craved one particular treasure.

As a child, I had everything I longed for. The villagers knew Mogra had a daughter, and if they brought something for me, a beautiful piece of jewelry or a gown, she would take it favorably. I must confess I was very spoiled, but it was not entirely my doing. My mother's fondness for beautiful things caused it.

I remember one of my requests very clearly. An old man came to our house one evening, his back bent and his brown face weathered and burnt by the sun. He was poor, but had somehow managed to get his hands on a small golden circlet. When my mother opened the door and saw the circlet, her lips curved upward greedily.

"What would you like?" she asked, never one for fanciful words.

"I need a healing draught," said the old man. His face held a mixture of fear and hope. I peered out at him from behind my mother's skirt, studying his face. All people who came to our house interested me, but I never saw the same person twice. Except for the visitors who came to trade, I was kept in complete isolation.

My mother thought about it. I knew she wanted the circlet. Her trembling fingers and wide eyes gave her away. With a richer customer, she might have pushed for more, but the man was giving her all he had. "Who is it for?"

"My son's young daughter. She's been ill for months."

"What are her symptoms?"

They talked for a few moments about things I did not understand, and my mother hurried back into the house. I trailed behind her, holding bunches of her soft, white skirt in my hands. She walked into the kitchen, heading toward the magic door. "Herb closet, please," she said, tapping three times to rouse the door. It swung open, and I followed her inside.

The dark, narrow herb closet had four walls, all shelved. Each level was crowded with baskets of herbs. My mother dug into some of the baskets, selecting the leaves and roots that she wanted. I knew some of the herbs, since she had already begun teaching me the art of healing and poisoning. She talked to me whenever she made her potions.

"First, valerian root to put her to sleep. Then, belladonna to take away her pain. Use only the root, Ailynn," she said as she dug into the basket. "Occasionally the leaves, but never touch the berries. They are deadly poisonous." I had heard that mantra before, mostly because my mother wanted to be sure I would not be tempted to eat them. She dug out a thick, fleshy white root with her hands and passed it to me before hurrying over to another shelf. "And aconite, my darling, to calm the girl's fever and pulse, but it must be prepared specially. It is also a poison."

"Mother, why are so many of your healing plants poisonous?"

"Because poisons are powerful," she said. "Even wormwort, one of the strongest herbs we use to cleanse the body, can only be taken in the smallest of doses before it kills you. Poisons manipulate the body, and if you harness their power correctly, the world can be yours." I did not understand her then, but those words stayed in my mind well through adulthood. Although many of her other lessons were faulty, I never doubted anything Mother taught me about plants.

Once she had collected the leaves and roots she wanted, she hurried into the kitchen and began crumbling and chopping, teaching me all the while. My mother had many flaws—her greed, her pride, her overconfidence—but she was wise, and she did try and do a little good back then, as long as she received payment.

After a while, she finished both a draught and a cream for the old man and carried them out to him where he waited at the door. Mother never allowed people into her house, and everyone knew she would hex anyone who invaded her privacy. She gave him the cream and the draught and told him what dosages to give. Then, he handed her the circlet. With a nod of her head, she bid him farewell and closed the door, placing the circlet on my head.

"I love you. You are my princess," she said, stroking my cheek as she knelt down to my level. "My beautiful girl, and you shall have anything that you want."

"Can the old man's granddaughter come and play with me when she is well?" I asked.

At that age, I had already tired of the many treasures my mother hoarded. The beautiful gowns and the precious jewels had grown dull. Lately, I thought more about the people who came to our house. I wondered what they knew, what their mothers were like, and whether they would like me. The shiny new toys they brought were nice to look at, but what I wanted most of all was a friend.

Mother did not answer. Instead, she stood up and headed outside to work in her garden. "Go and play downstairs," she ordered, but I could tell that her mind was elsewhere.

* * *

Days blended together in our house. Mother's lessons kept me busy, but my feelings of discontent grew, and I know she sensed it. Sometimes, in the afternoon, she would stand in her garden amongst her herbs, looking to the sky. I learned later she had been thinking about how to find me a suitable playmate. It would not have been appropriate for me to mingle with the village children of my age, but I

3

was lonely. She could not be at peace until I was happy again.

My next clear memory was of a crisp night in autumn. I sat on my mother's lap by the fire in the kitchen as she told me a story and braided my hair. The warmth of the flames and my mother's voice had just started lulling me to sleep when a muffled yelp drifted in from outside. Mother looked over her shoulder and out a nearby window, her chin tilting up as she listened harder. Someone was in the back garden.

"Stay here, Ailynn." She hurried to the door while I sat on the rug next to the fire. As soon as she was out of sight, I scrambled up to the window, peeking over the sill so no one could see me. Everything was quiet for a few moments, and then I saw my mother again. Her face glowed in the moonlight, and she held onto a thin man by the back of his shirt. She seemed as tall as an oak tree standing in front of the intruder, angry and fierce, just as the villagers whispered she was. "Why you dare to descend into my garden and steal my rampion?"

The man tried to speak, but only a small, strangled cry came out from between his trembling lips. I had seen the frightened, awed looks of the people who came to bargain with Mother, but none of them seemed this afraid. I had never seen her this angry before, either. I knew her garden was precious to her, but her fury still shocked me.

"Ah, let mercy be taking the place of justice," the man stammered. "I had to!" His accent was familiar, the same one used by the local villagers, but it still sounded strange to my ears. Mother and I had always spoken differently, and to me, his words seemed like they were in all the wrong places.

"You had to?" Mother repeated. Her voice frosted, each word a shard of ice. She threw him to the ground, and he remained there, cringing away from her.

"My wife is carrying our first child, and she was craving rampion. You know if a mother isn't having the food she desires, the baby is cursed."

Her mood turned thoughtful, and she looked once more at the man cowering by her feet. "If it is as you say, then you may take away as much rampion as you like. I will even spare your life and tend to the arm you injured when you fell over my wall. It is probably broken, and the tissue is starting to swell. I mark only one condition."

"Anything, Mistress."

"You must bring me the child your wife will bear. I will attend to the birthing myself. Your wife will not die in her childbed. But I will raise

4

the girl, and she will want for nothing."

The man's face twisted in horror. "You would take my daughter from me?" He scrambled further back on the ground. "Never!"

Mother narrowed her eyes. "If you do not give her to me, I will curse your entire family after I kill you for stealing my rampion. Think on it. This way, your daughter will have everything she could ever dream of possessing." I caught a glimpse of her nose wrinkling with disgust. "From the looks of your clothes, you cannot provide her with much."

"But my only child…"

Mother's voice softened. "You will have more children, as many you please. I will be midwife for the others as well. I require no payment except for your daughter. I promise you she will come to no harm." She paused, and her soothing voice took on a harder edge. "Besides, if you don't give her to me, I will simply take her. And you and your wife will both be barren."

She had backed the man into a corner. He had no other choice. I was too young to understand just how threatening my mother's offer was, but I recognized the wide-eyed look of terror on the man's face. "Take her, then," he said. "Just give me the rampion, and I'll be on my way."

"After I heal your arm," Mother insisted. She grabbed the man's healthy shoulder and dragged him toward the house. Mother always had a price for everything. She was not above using threats and fear to get what she wanted, but she was not entirely evil back then. Along with the fear most villagers felt toward her, a measure of respect lingered there as well.

I hurried back to the fireplace and closed my eyes, pretending I had fallen asleep on the rug, but my mother was not fooled. "Up with you, Ailynn," she said as soon as she came inside. I got to my feet, and she pulled me against her belly while the man waited by the door, afraid to step inside the house. "Which herbs would you use for a swelling, dear heart?"

I remembered the cream we had made for the old man several weeks before. "Aconite?"

"That will do. Fetch me some for a poultice, and bring water to put over the fire."

I hurried to do as she asked, my hands shaking with excitement as I ran to the small wooden door. "Herb room, please," I said, but my thoughts were elsewhere. I was going to have a friend. Someone to play games with and tell secrets to. Someone to take care of. Exactly what I had wanted. I knew my mother had forced the man to give up his daughter for me, and, selfishly, I loved her for it. I didn't know then just how much a parent might miss their child.

CHAPTER TWO

THE BABY CAME TO live with us a little over a month later. When Mother first brought her home, her face was bright red, and she squalled like the kittens Diath, Mother's cat, had given birth to beneath our house. But I knew this girl, my new present, was nothing like a kitten. She would grow to walk and talk, and someday she would be able to play with me.

Mother walked over to an intricately carved wooden chair, payment for one of her spells, and sat down. The baby wriggled in her wrappings, pushing at them with her tiny fists.

"May I see her?" I asked, reaching up to pull aside the blanket.

Mother moved my hands away. "Be patient, Ailynn. I have to feed her first. She is very hungry, and she is weak after coming into the world."

"Will we need a wet nurse?" Most other children my age understood little about babies, but my mother was a healer, and children often took ill, especially the very small ones. Several women came to our house with sick newborns, and many more asked for herbs from Mother's garden to help them feed their babies.

"I will nurse her myself. I don't want anyone else in my house. I've been taking the herbs I need for several days, and I already have milk for her." She removed her cloak and handed it to me. "Put this away, please, Ailynn. Then, you can come and see your new playmate."

"But if we're going to keep her, doesn't that mean she's my sister?"

Mother paused. I could tell the question bothered her, although I wasn't sure why. "No," she said at last. "She is not your sister. You must let me tell her about her real parents when she's old enough. Do you understand?"

I nodded. "Yes." Sometimes, I wonder if Mother intentionally kept me from thinking of her as my sister because she could predict what would happen as the years passed, or if she simply considered the baby to be another one of her treasures. She rarely shared her thoughts with me.

"Good girl. Now, enough of your questions. Go and do what I told you."

I dashed off to put her cloak away, eager to get back to the new baby as quickly as possible. "Hush, Ailynn," Mother said when I skidded back into the room. "She's finally stopped crying." She had pulled down her shirt to let the baby nurse. I was even more excited to see her now that she had stopped wailing loud enough to wake the dead.

"She's so small," I whispered, staring at the child with wide eyes. "Was I that small once?"

Mother smiled. "Oh, you were smaller still. You came several weeks before you were supposed to. I went days without sleep trying to keep you alive. This child will be much easier to care for."

"May I help feed her when she is older?"

"Of course. You are going to have to help me be responsible for her, and see that she grows up to be as healthy and beautiful as you are."

I reached out to stroke the baby's head. She had surprisingly thick hair for a newborn, and her head was covered with beautiful golden curls. Mother's smile widened. "Yes, I noticed that, too. Perhaps the rampion her father took from my garden might have something to do with it. I've seen stranger things."

"Does she have a name?" I asked.

"No," Mother said. "Would you like to name her, Ailynn?"

I looked at the baby carefully, trying to decide on a good name. "What if we named her after the rampion her father took?"

Mother's eyebrows lifted. "You want to name the child rampion?"

"No, but you've taught me that plants have many different names. Is there another name for rampion?"

Mother leaned back in the chair and gave me a thoughtful look as she cradled the baby against her chest. "Rampion is a flowering plant. The old Amendyrri word for blossom is 'raisa.' Would that do?"

"Raisa," I said, trying the name on my tongue. I smiled up at the child and nodded my head. "It's a pretty name."

8

"Very pretty. And our Raisa will grow up pretty, too."

"Will she look like her mother as I look like you?"

"Yes. Most daughters look like their mothers or their fathers. Her mother has these same golden curls." She tugged at one fondly, curling it around her finger. The baby squirmed for a moment, then went back to nursing.

An idea struck me. "Mother, may I give Raisa a gift?"

"Of course."

With her blessing, I ran to the small wooden door. "Treasure room, please." The door was tired, and I waited anxiously in front of it for several seconds before scurrying into the treasure room. I brushed past the dresses and tapestries, hunting for the golden circlet the old man had given to me. I found it sitting on top of a sheet of fine glass. I picked it up slowly, careful not to bend or dirty the soft metal. Even though the room was cold, it felt warm in my hands.

I hurried back through the door and returned to Mother with the circlet in my grip. Raisa was fast asleep on her lap. "Look, Ailynn, you can see her face now," she said, brushing aside the baby's curls.

I reached out and took Raisa's hand in mine, opening her small fingers and closing them around the circlet. She pulled it close to her chest, but her eyes remained shut. "I love you. You are my princess," I whispered, repeating the words Mother had said when she had given me the circlet. "My beautiful girl, and you shall have anything that you want."

* * *

Raisa was dearer to me than any of my mother's treasures. As she grew, so did our bond, and we were nearly inseparable by the time she reached childhood. Her first word was my name, "Ayn." She could not pronounce it properly with her baby tongue, but it still touched me. Even though I was four years older, neither of us seemed to mind the age difference. I enjoyed playing with her and teaching her, and she enjoyed learning.

I told her stories by candlelight in the evenings, and eventually taught her to read them herself. I kept her entertained with shows of light, which I could conjure in my hands. I helped her run through the forest and climb trees, and I was always there to patch up any scrape or bruise. I taught her to recognize the birds by sight and song, and with my knowledge of plants, I made sure she always knew which were safe to eat and which were poisonous.

As Raisa learned, so did I. By the time I was ten, Mother started allowing me to help her prepare the herbs she used, and sometimes she would let me make simple healing draughts and potions by myself. My education expanded in other ways. Magic flowed in my blood, and when Mother first noticed me playing with the fire of a candle and bending it to my will, she began teaching me in earnest. I was *Ariada*—a witch—just as she was, and she spent many long hours showing me her secrets and teaching me Words of Power.

"There are seven types of magic," she told me, "but ours is by far the most powerful, more powerful than the Shamans, the Druids, and even the Shapers. Witches are children of the First Son, an *Ariada* whose will was so strong he could bring rain down from the sky and burn entire cities to dust. When you master Words of Power, when you master the elements instead of kneeling before them, you will master the world itself."

Of all the elements I learned to whisper with, fire soon became my favorite. Since fire eats everything it touches, it was not difficult to draw it out of whatever I chose, even my own flesh. But fire requires sacrifice. As the burns on my hands grew, I became very adept at making poultices. Soon, the Words I needed fell as naturally from my tongue as my own name.

Raisa was not interested magic, and her few failed attempts showed she was not *Ariada*, but she had a wonderful imagination. She would often make up stories while my mother and I worked. She had a voice as light and golden as her hair, and Mother and I loved to listen to her sing. We taught her all the songs we knew, and when we ran out, she made up new ones. When she adopted a kitten from another of Diath's litters, she named him Sing.

Despite the strange events that brought her to us, Raisa was an ordinary child except for one thing. The beautiful curls she had been born with grew quickly and did not stop at her waist. From her second birthday on, her golden hair trailed on the ground. My mother tried all of her herbs and charms, but nothing could make the hair stop growing. I was given the task of cutting it to her shoulders every day, a chore I did not mind.

By age six, Raisa began asking questions about things she had noticed. "Why do you and your mother have auburn hair when mine is golden?" she asked one evening while I brushed her curls.

"What does it matter? Your hair is beautiful the way it is. Come on, let's go and try on some of the clothes in the treasure rooms. You can be one of the characters in your stories." And so I diverted her questions. She knew my mother, whom she called Mother Gothel, was not her blood, and that I was not her sister, but not much more. I couldn't bring myself to tell her she had been taken away from her real parents, and I dreaded the day when she would ask me directly. If she did, I knew the truth would come spilling out.

But even though I could not find the strength to lie to Raisa, Mother could. Her questions finally came to a head one evening. Raisa enjoyed reading even at a young age, and she flipped through one of her fairytale books by the fireplace in the kitchen while Mother and I worked. I cut the herbs and crushed them into a fine powder while Mother poured the correct dosages into a draught. But Raisa's voice floated across the room, interrupting our work. "Do I have a mother?"

I looked over my shoulder, staring into her wide, curious brown eyes. I silently pleaded she would let the question drop, or Mother would dismiss her, but something told me neither of us could put her off any longer.

"Why do you ask?" Mother said, sprinkling a handful of powder into a measuring jar.

"I just want to know. Please tell me."

"You had a mother and father," she admitted. "All babies come from a mother and father, but sometimes they don't live with them. You know that."

"Then how did I come here?" Raisa asked.

This time, Mother did not hesitate. "The forest gave you to us. One night in summer, Ailynn and I heard something crying near the garden. You were a newborn then, and we decided to take you in and raise you as our own. I was waiting to tell you until you were older, but six is old enough, I suppose."

I feared Raisa would not believe the lie, but slowly, her face softened in the light of the fire. My dread was replaced with the slow, sinking feeling of guilt. By remaining silent, I was complicit in Mother's deception. "Why didn't you tell me sooner, Mother Gothel?" she asked, sounding only slightly upset.

Mother left the counter and leaned down to kiss the top of Raisa's head. "I was waiting until you were old enough to understand."

I returned to slicing sneezewort leaves, afraid that Raisa might see the truth in my eyes. My hands shook, and I nearly cut myself twice.

That ended Raisa's stream of questions about her past. Part of me was relieved Mother had fixed the problem so neatly, but another, deeper part of me felt guilty about the lie. The falsehood began to eat at me from the inside out even though I had not been the one to tell it. Eventually I learned to ignore the hurt, but the feelings of shame were still there, buried deep inside of me.

CHAPTER THREE

GROWING UP ISOLATED FROM the rest of the world, I did not any opportunities to make friends. Raisa's company was such a joy to me. She was not like a sister, but far more than just a playmate. She was mine, and that was all that mattered. However, I did have the opportunity to meet another child my own age just after my eleventh birthday.

The summer rain drummed on the roof, and Raisa sat in front of the kitchen window. Her mood was always bright, even in foul weather. She giggled as the raindrops raced each other down the clear glass surface and followed them with her finger.

"No," I said, pulling her hands away from the glass. "You might smudge it. Come away from the window, and we can play the fairytale game."

The fairytale game was Raisa's favorite. We dressed up in clothes, jewelry, and armor from my mother's treasure rooms and pretended to be the heroes from many of Amendyr's famous stories. The tales of our kingdom fascinated her, and she never went to bed without hiding one of Mother's books under the covers.

We often had to play multiple roles at one time, but I did not mind at all. We had been knights, old wizards, giant dragons, cunning thieves, burly dwarves, and even Liarre, the half-human, half-animal creations of Lir the Shaper. I was not much of an actress, but Raisa usually found ways to improve on my narration. Once she knew the story, she took over.

My favorite stories were the ones about *Tuathe*, lovers who shared a bond so strong nothing could sever it, not even death. The word meant 'we two that are one' in the ancient Amendyrri language, and I was not surprised it had survived for so many generations. Secretly, I hoped Raisa and I would be *Tuathe* when we grew up.

We played the fairytale game for a candle mark before I realized Mother was not in the house. At first, I assumed she was in one of the rooms behind the magical door, perhaps the library. When she did not emerge, I began to wonder, and then I began to worry. I was used to looking after Raisa by myself, but being alone for such a long period of time made me uneasy. She did not usually leave us without an explanation.

Raisa abandoned the game to stand beside me. She took my hand, looking up at me with trusting eyes. "Ailynn, what are you worrying about?"

"Nothing. I was just wondering where Mother went."

Before we could start playing again, the front door slammed open with a loud crash, as though a violent wind had blown it against the wall. Mother stood silhouetted in the doorway, tall and draped in her heavy black cloak. She held it closed at the neck to protect her face from the rain. Another figure stood beside her, and I realized with some excitement that it was another child.

"Ailynn," Mother called, holding open her arms and letting go of the child's hand. I ran to hug her, and the cold rain sloughing from her cloak soaked into my clothes. The strange child was a boy, and not a very impressive one at that. His wet blonde hair was plastered to his forehead, and his nose curved up a little at the tip. He looked me up and down, making a similarly unfavorable judgment.

Although he was not much to look at, I was as interested in him as he seemed to be in me. I did not get many opportunities to interact with children besides Raisa. "Arim dei," I said, letting go of my mother to wave at the boy. "My name is Ailynn. What's yours?"

He did not return the greeting. "Byron Wylean-James the Third," he said, reaching up to wipe his nose with his sleeve. Water dripped off his face, and he had no cloak to keep off the rain. He had a partially Serian name and, judging by his accent, I suspected he lived near the border like us. He looked longingly inside the house, and I stepped back from the doorway to give him and Mother more room.

"Why are you here, Byron?" I asked, also directing the question at Mother. She hesitated, undoing the clasp of her cloak and drawing down the hood. Her hair spilled out around her shoulders, and she avoided my gaze. Usually, she did not hesitate to answer my questions. Suspicion choked up my throat.

"Byron will be visiting us for a little while, Princess. And how is my other girl? Come here." She knelt down so Raisa, who had decided it was safe enough to come forward, could give her a hug as well.

"I'm bored," Byron said, and the nasal tone of his voice made me scrunch up my face. Now that the attention was back on him, he seemed content to keep it that way. "When do I get to eat? Where are the servants?"

"Servants?" I looked skeptically around the cottage. Where did he expect us to keep servants in a place like this?

"Yes, servants. Where are they? They haven't come to bring us dry clothes yet."

My disbelief rapidly shifted into annoyance. "Why do you need servants for that? You've got two hands and two legs."

He opened his mouth as if to complain again, but before he could continue whining, Raisa let go of Mother and ran over to tug at his sleeve. "Do you want to play the fairytale game with us?"

Byron looked at her sourly. He began to shake his head, but Mother gave him a small push in the middle of his back, forcing him toward us. "That sounds like a good idea. Go occupy yourself with Ailynn and Raisa, Byron. I need to get in touch with your father and tell him where you are so he can make arrangements."

So Byron would be staying for the duration, not just an hour or two until the storm let up. My lips pulled into a frown. As appealing as a new playmate might have seemed at first, I was annoyed that he had barged into my house unannounced and proceeded to judge everything about it, and me, with only a glance.

"We were doing Reagan and Saweya this time," I said when it became obvious my mother planned to leave us to our own devices. "Maybe you can be the knight that comes to rescue Saweya from the tower?"

"I'm Saweya," Raisa interrupted, showing off the golden circlet she wore on her head, the same one I had presented to her on the night she came to stay with us. "She was the seventh daughter of the seventh king of Amendyr, but she left Kalmarin when—"

"A princess. All right. I don't need a history lesson," Byron interrupted, obviously unimpressed by Raisa's knowledge. He turned toward me and narrowed his eyes. "And who are you supposed to be? That cloak looks like you pulled it out from a cleaning bucket."

I sighed and held the edges of the cloak out with my hands, letting it fall down past my arms like the sails of a dragon's wings. "I'm Reagan." Byron only stared at me. He did not recognize the name. "The dragon. Don't you know the story? Maybe you should have listened to Raisa after all."

He shrugged. "I don't have time for stories. My father does important things."

"That's all right. I can tell it," Raisa said, not put off in the slightest by Byron's rude behavior. "I sing of Saweya, the seventh daughter of the seventh king of Amendyr. Greed clouded her father's heart, and when she was only a child, he trapped her high in a tower..."

The game went well at first. I played Reagan, the dragon that circled Saweya's tower to protect her from knights errant. In the original story, she was actually female, although later Serian retellings edited that part out. Reagan was not a true dragon, but a human cursed to change form whenever the tower needed to be protected. Over time, she fell in love with her captive. Reagan offered to let Saweya go, but Saweya decided to stay on the condition that she could occasionally leave the tower. During one of her journeys, her evil father's emissaries kidnapped her and returned her to his palace at Kalmarin, the shining city on the southern cliffs. Saweya used her own cunning to escape, while Reagan found the strength to break the magical bindings tying her to the tower. In a blood-rage, she destroyed the king's palace. At least, that is how the story was supposed to go.

Byron entered on his cue, playing the knight as his first role. I had also offered to let him play the king later in the story, even though I sometimes liked being the villain. He wore a helmet far too big for his head and a swirling silk cloak, and he held a silver dirk with a jeweled hilt in his left hand. Except for the dirk, I thought he looked rather ridiculous, but he seemed to think the props made him dashing. I decided not to correct his assumption.

"Ho, dragon," he hollered, waving the blade around in a threatening manner. "Come out and face me." He was actually doing well in his role despite his over-large helmet, and I gave him an encouraging smile.

"Run," I roared. "Run, or I will feast upon your pathetic carcass and leave your bones to bleach in the sun." Bearing imaginary claws and teeth, I lunged at him and began the fight. I had to be careful of his wild swings. Unlike the real Reagan, I had no leathery hide or claws to protect me.

"Okay," I said, swiping at him with my hand. "Now you have to die."

Byron lowered the dirk, frowning. "I don't want to die. The knight should win the fight."

"That's not how the story goes. Besides, you're still playing. You get to be the evil king, too."

Byron stood his ground, crossing his arms over his chest. "No. The knight should always win the fight and rescue the princess." He gestured at Raisa, who wrinkled her brow.

I narrowed my eyes. "Your parents only raised you on Serian fairy-stories, then. I'm not going to change it just because you don't like how it goes."

"Then I'll change it. I challenge you to mortal combat." Byron tightened his grip around the handle of the dirk. This time, when he raised it to slash at me, I decided not to play easy with him.

I pulled at the rush of my blood, fed from the living heat burning beneath my skin, and thrust my palm down. "Fel!" Sparks flew up from the floor, gathering around my hand in a flickering cloud. Spiced smoke filled my nose, and the remnants of the Word of Power burned on my tongue, but I smiled at the pain. If I was going to be a dragon, I would play the role properly.

Byron took one look at the flame playing between my fingers and stumbled back, raising his arm to protect his face. The dirk clattered onto the floorboards. "You're—you're *Ariada*! Get away from me. My father says your kind is evil and twisted."

I stepped forward. "Your father says that? Perhaps he isn't as wise as you think."

Byron glared at me from beneath his oversized helmet, torn between fear and anger. "My father is a very important man. Byron Wylean-James the Second—"

"If you like him so much, why are you here instead of at home?" I muttered.

"I don't know, *Ariada*." On his Serian lips, the word sounded a curse. "Your mother just took me away."

My eyes widened, and I let the heat licking at my palms die away. "My mother took you?" Had I heard him correctly?

"Yes." Byron looked relieved once the fire was gone, but he still kept a cautious distance. "It happened once before. Father says that bad people sometimes take the children of important men like him and ask for gold to give them back. He said it's called a ransom."

"My mother is ransoming you?"

"Yes," Byron said. "She told me if my father gives her what she asks for, she'll send me back and nothing bad will happen. It didn't the last time, so I'm not worried. She knows better than to hurt someone like me. My father will come after her if she does. He just thinks paying the gold is easier."

I couldn't believe it. I had never thought Mother capable of kidnapping a nobleman's son. Perhaps it shouldn't have surprised me so much. She had been greedy enough to take Raisa away from her parents, after all, even though it had been for my sake. How was that any different than stealing a nobleman's son and trading him back for gold? "I don't think we should play anymore."

Fortunately, Mother saved me the trouble of finding an excuse to leave the room. "Ailynn," she called out. "Come into the kitchen and help me." I hurried away, leaving Raisa and Byron behind.

I did not mention what Byron had said to Mother that night, or the next morning when she took him away. When she returned, she carried with her several bags of gold, a diamond tiara, a full set of chain mail armor, and a beautifully decorated shield. I did not ask her where the new presents had come from. I did not want to know.

CHAPTER FOUR

MOTHER'S RELATIONSHIP WITH RAISA was different than mine. Although she took great pride in Raisa's accomplishments and offered praise as Raisa devoured all of the history books in the library, she was otherwise reserved with her words. Occasionally she offered Raisa a hug or a smile, but I noticed a certain distance to her affections. It was not until Raisa turned fifteen that I finally understood why.

We made our way through the forest late one afternoon, searching for Sing at Raisa's request. He had grown into a sleek, well-fed cat over the years, and he had a special affection for her. If she had shown any magical aptitude at all, I would have suspected them of being bonded like my mother was with Diath. But he was an ordinary pet, aside from his uncanny ability to get himself in trouble.

It was autumn again, Raisa's favorite time of year, and the trees beyond our cottage had started to shed their leaves. She loved the colors and the smell of the coming frost, and her descriptions were so vivid I could not help but love them, too. "See how the maple leaves look like wide brown hands," she said to me that evening, pointing at a fresh pile below a tall maple tree.

"They are giants' hands, reaching out to grab you," I teased, coming up behind her and tickling her sides. She squealed and wriggled to get out of my arms, but I held her fast until she stilled. I pulled her close for a moment, my lips resting a breath away from her hair, and then let her go, trying to ignore my racing heart. Over the past year, my feelings for Raisa had changed, and I still wasn't sure what to make of them.

"Here," I said, pulling away and gesturing down one of the hidden forest paths. "You look for him along there, and I'll go the other way. We'll find him faster if we split up. We'll meet back by the maple tree."

"All right, Ailynn," she said. She grabbed my hand, standing on tiptoe to kiss my cheek. My face flushed with heat, and I was glad when she ran off without noticing.

I spent the next several minutes looking for Sing, but did not find him. I finally stopped beside a slender ash tree and peered up into its branches, trying to decide whether the black spot above my head was a bird's nest or the curled body of a sleeping cat. Before I could get a closer look, a loud scream rose above the forest noises. My heart stopped. It had to be Raisa. Who else would dare travel here this close to sunset?

I ran in the direction of the sound, grateful I knew the forest floor well enough to cross in near-dark without falling. Raisa screamed again, and I adjusted my course, leaving the path and weaving between the trees. At last, I rushed into a small glade. The hulking back of a man rose above me. He was as large as a bear and looked to be about as strong. I could not see much past his bulk, but I caught a glimpse of golden hair over his shoulder. His hand wrapped around Raisa's throat.

I did not think. I did not even need to speak my Word Of Power. The cold, yawning emptiness of fear ripped open in my chest, and from that pit of nothingness came fire. I forgot the leaves at my feet and gave of my flesh instead. Flames lashed from my fingertips, and the man screamed as the fire ate into his back. He dropped Raisa and twisted, toppling to the ground and writhing over the leaves. The leaves went up in smoke, and he along with them, yelling loud enough to shatter the sky.

I grabbed Raisa with my free hand and hoisted her to her feet, clutching her arm and dragging her away through the trees. The dying shouts of the man followed behind us for several hundred yards until we were well away. Neither of us stopped running until we reached Mother's house.

"What happened?" she asked as we stumbled in through the door. "Ailynn, your hands are burned, and Raisa, your dress is torn."

I nearly wept when I saw my Raisa clutching her dress together. It had been ripped down the front. "I don't understand," she cried, hurrying into my arms. "What happened?"

"Hush, dear heart," I whispered, rocking her against my chest. "You're safe."

Raisa might not have understood what had happened, but Mother did. "Did you get there in time?" she asked coldly, staring out of the window.

"Yes," I said. Raisa's tears stained the shoulder of my dress, and I stroked her tangled curls, trying to calm her down as her body trembled against mine. "She's alive, isn't she?" It wasn't what Mother had meant, but it was the thing that mattered most to me.

Mother's next question almost made me sick. "Did you finish him?"

"Yes." The word did not come easily. I had never killed anyone before. Had I killed the man? Perhaps he was still writhing on the forest floor, crumbling away to ash. "At least, I think I did."

Mother looked down at my raw hands and shook her head. "And you didn't think to check? I suspect you forgot to put the fire out as well." I lowered my eyes in shame. "Take Raisa to bed. Don't let her out of your sight. I'll be back once I've made sure he's dead and our home isn't going to burn down." She stormed out of the back door, not even bothering to grab a cloak.

Once she had left, I scooped Raisa into my arms and carried her to into her bedroom. Sing, who had found his way back home without our help, uncurled from the foot of the bed and made room for the two of us. I set Raisa down on top of the sheets and left her there. She wept silently as I hurried to the closet, but the tears came harder as I lifted the torn dress away and slipped a fresh nightgown over her head. Finally, she fell back on the bed and drifted off to sleep, holding Sing in her arms while she rested in mine. I remained awake, waiting for Mother to return.

She was gone all through the night and did not come back to the cottage until high noon the next morning. Raisa still rested, and I remained at her side even when I heard the sound of footsteps outside the bedroom door. It opened a crack, and Mother's face peered in at me. "How is she, Ailynn?"

"Still sleeping." I brushed her hair away from her face, and it was heavier than usual against my hand. She had fallen asleep before I could cut it. "She hasn't woken since last night. Perhaps it's for the best."

"Come with me," Mother said. Her tone made it clear that she would not tolerate disobedience.

I unwove my arms from around Raisa's body as slowly as I could and bent down to kiss her head. The cat opened one eye and watched me as I stood. I crept away, slipping into the next room without moving the door so the hinges would not creak.

Mother hurried me over to the kitchen table and forced me to sit. I

21

wilted against the back of my chair, completely drained of energy. I
heard the sound of water being poured, but could not summon the
strength to turn my head. My eyes remained fixed on the wall until
Mother set a warm mug of tea in front of me. I began to refuse, but she
held up her hand. "Drink your tea, Ailynn, and listen to me."

My hands shook with fatigue and fear, but I lifted the tea to my
lips, clutching the cup tight so it would not tremble. The warm drink was
strong, and it wasn't one of Mother's usual brews. My body tingled with
warmth, and some of the tiredness left me. "I took care of the man,"
Mother said, "as well as your little accident. You must be more careful
with Words of Power. You know how to use them, but you still don't
know how to control them."

I glared at her over the rim of my cup. The unnatural calmness in
her voice grated on my nerves. "I don't think this is the right time for a
magic lesson, Mother. Raisa could have been hurt, maybe even killed. I
did what I had to." My brief regret over taking a life had vanished
sometime during the night. I much preferred my righteous anger to the
nauseating feelings of guilt.

"He will not bother anyone again, but that won't stop others from
trying. Raisa is a beautiful woman."

I frowned. "And simply being beautiful gives someone else the right
to hurt her? That is the most ridiculous thing I have ever heard."

Mother shook her head. "I never said it was right or fair. I have
kept you both hidden away from the world for a reason. There are
people in it who love to destroy beauty and goodness, no matter what
form it takes. They have always existed, and they will continue to exist
as long as humans draw breath."

The cold bite of fear crept over me. Mother had planned
something. I could tell just by looking at her. Whatever it was, I knew I
would not like it. "She is only fifteen," I protested. "She is still a child."

"A girl of fifteen is hardly a child. Girls in the village begin thinking
of marriage at that age, and you had memorized all the poisons in my
garden and stopped needing to speak your Words of Power aloud. Raisa
cannot defend herself as you can. She is not *Ariada*."

"But I am. I can protect her."

Mother crossed her arms over her chest. "How? By nearly burning
down the forest?"

I stared down into my teacup. "Then what do you suggest we do?"

"I have called in several old debts. There is a cave about half an
hour's walk from the house. I'm sure I can make it comfortable

enough."

My eyes narrowed. "For what purpose?" I asked, although I already knew.

"For Raisa's protection, of course. As long as she lives here with us, she will remain attached to the outside world, as well as all the dangers it holds."

I leapt to my feet, nearly sending my chair crashing to the floor. "What? You would keep her hidden away like the rest of your treasures? She'll go mad." I shook with rage, listening to my own words echo in my head. That was when I understood. Mother loved Raisa, but not as I did. The greedy part of her saw only another bauble, a fetching toy she had to hide lest someone steal or break it. "The man is dead. Raisa isn't in any danger. I will not allow this."

Mother remained in her chair, unmoved by my display of anger. "I am not seeking your permission, Ailynn. More people will always come. They will bring their evil with them. Raisa will stay in the cave for her own protection. Someday, you will thank me for keeping her safe."

I stepped forward, determined to confront her, but my legs shook beneath me. I had to grip the edge of the table to steady myself. "I won't..." Getting up had been a mistake. I sank back into my chair, blinking to clear my blurry eyes as Mother stood. She handed the cup of tea back to me and curled her fingers around my shoulder.

"Finish your tea, Ailynn, and then get some rest. Things will seem better tomorrow."

I did not have it in me to fight her. Obediently, I took another sip of tea, closing my eyes as the warm brew curled around my tongue and slid down my throat. I would never be able to talk Mother out of her crazy idea, at least not this way. Despite how wrong she was about everything else, I needed to follow her first piece of advice and exercise self-control. "When will you take her away?"

"A few weeks. It will give me time to prepare and allow both of you to grow accustomed to the idea." Her hand moved up from my shoulder, stroking my hair in a rare gesture of affection. My stomach twisted into knots. "I promise, nothing will change," she murmured. "You may stay with her as often as you like, and I'll make sure she has Sing and all of her favorite books to keep her company when you're gone."

"Of course," I said, but my mind was elsewhere. A few weeks. If Mother told the truth, I would have more than enough time to come up with a plan.

Rae D. Magdon

CHAPTER FIVE

FOR A FEW HOURS each day, Mother left me to watch Raisa while she went to prepare the cave. It was the only time both of us were not with her. When she did come home, she brooded, pacing the house like a wolf guarding its kill. I did my best to ignore her, staring at blank spaces on the wall and trying to come up with a plan. Raisa never complained, but I could tell she was just as unhappy as I was. She had always been perceptive, and my fears seeped into her. She took food only when I made her, and her sleep grew fitful.

I tried to be a steady source of comfort to her. I held her more than usual and stroked her hair as she rested her head in my lap. I stopped cutting it, and when Raisa asked why, I told her that Mother would explain in a few weeks. I still despised the idea of imprisoning Raisa, but aside from running away, I couldn't think of another solution Mother would accept. Her extreme paranoia grew worse. She glanced out the window at least once an hour to make sure no one was outside.

Raisa's changes were more difficult to bear. The beautiful, laughing child full of stories faded into a shadow of herself, and all of her smiles disappeared. She spent most of her time crying. Patches of my shirt were soaked with her tears more often than not. Raisa understood why the man had attacked her, but she did not know why Mother had acted so harshly. Yet she did not ask questions, either, something I was thankful for. I was not sure if I would be able to explain it to her. Sing also sensed something was very wrong. He stayed close to his mistress, tailing Raisa like a faithful dog as she wandered from room to room and curling up with us as we sat in front of the fire.

After only two tedious weeks, Mother declared that the cave was ready. She took me to see it one night, but not before making sure the house was sealed up tight behind us. Reluctantly, I followed her out into the forest. It was well past sunset, and only hints of silvery moonlight streaked through the thick canopy of autumn leaves. Insects buzzed from their hiding places in the tree branches, and the other night sounds almost covered our footfalls as we walked silently over the wet ground.

At last, we reached a small ledge of rock beside a large oak tree. Tucked just beneath, hidden in such a way that it could only be seen from the perfect angle, was the black, gaping maw of a cave. I squinted down into the darkness, but I could not make out anything past the entrance. The grey stones surrounding the cave were cracked, covered with moss and lichen. "You aged them?"

Mother followed my gaze and nodded. "It looked strange with fresh-cut stones. New rock in such an ancient forest would be too noticeable." She stepped toward the entrance to the cave. "Come. The way will change soon."

"What do you mean, the way will change?"

"I meant what I said. The tunnels are like the door at home. They change."

I nodded. That certainly explained why it had taken her so long to prepare Raisa's prison. "How am I supposed to find Raisa once you bring her here?"

"Her hair, of course. That is why I told you to stop cutting it."

My brow furrowed. "If the tunnels change, what happens to her hair?"

Mother smiled, but I could not bear to return the gesture. "I am a very good enchanter, Ailynn. I took that into account. Even if Raisa cuts her hair, it will grow again, and its edge will always find the sunlight. Now, enough questions. Follow me." She disappeared into the darkness, and despite my sense of foreboding, I had no choice but to follow.

The cave's slope was gradual, barely wide enough for two people to walk abreast. It smelled of limestone and black places, and I realized Mogra had created it with magic. A cave like this could not have formed in the middle of a forest, even this close to the Rengast Mountains. I moved forward carefully, afraid I might slip on the damp stone.

Soon, the weak starlight from the surface vanished. I murmured a Word of Power, letting the taste of pain break and crackle on my tongue. A small globe of light appeared in my hand, and I lifted it high, shining it on a fork in the tunnel. Both paths seemed endless. "Which way?"

Mother pointed to the left. "This way, at least until she arrives. Then, the stone will shift again."

We continued on for several minutes, turning so many times I could not possibly remember the way back. The faint hiss of the fire and my own unsteady breathing echoed from the cave walls. My stomach lurched. Once Mogra brought her here, Raisa would be utterly alone, trapped in this eerie silence forever. I quickened my pace, even more eager to reach our destination. I wanted to return to her as soon as possible.

At last, Mother came to a halt. Instead of dividing yet again, the passageway ended in a doorway. Mogra opened it, and we both stepped through. Beyond the door, the tunnel opened up into a spacious cavern. It was warm, unlike the rest of the cave, and although the walls and floor were made of stone, it had the appearance of a fully furnished room. A large canopied bed was tucked against one wall, and a tall bookshelf took up most of another. There were several tables and chairs in the middle of the room, and beside them was a clear fountain of water. Light shone down from somewhere above, and I lifted my eyes to see the stars. The ceiling only covered one portion of the ceiling.

Mogra stood beside me, looking up as well. "It's mostly an illusion, a window through the earth above us, but it serves its purpose. I didn't think it was fair to take the sky from her."

"Then let her stay with us," I pleaded, trying one last time to sway her. "No matter how comfortable you make this place, hiding her here would be cruel."

"Hiding her isn't foolish. It's merely practical."

The keen knife of anger twisted in my belly, but I kept a blank expression on my face, seething inwardly until the sharp edge of my rage had dulled. "When will you bring her?"

"Soon," she whispered. "The cave is nearly finished."

I turned away from the sky, unwilling to look up at the false stars any longer. "Take me home," I insisted. "I've seen enough."

She stared at me, lips parted as though she wanted to offer some justification, but she said nothing. Instead, she brushed past me and headed back into the darkness. I followed at a distance. I had endured Mother's moments of cruelty quietly over the years, but I could not ignore this.

Part of me never stopped loving her, but after that night, I never stopped hating her, either.

* * *

Raisa stirred as I sank back onto our bed, clutching at the sheets in her sleep. She tossed her head, her long twin braids curving through the folds in the covers like winding golden rivers. I stroked her cheek with the back of my hand, and her eyelids fluttered. She parted her lips slightly as she gazed up into my face. "Ailynn?"

"Sleep, dear heart," I whispered, feeling guilty I had awoken her.

"Where were you?" Her arms circled around me.

"It doesn't matter."

"Ailynn, where did you go?" she insisted.

"Mother took me out." The pleading look on her face made my chest tighten. I could not let this happen. We needed to escape as quickly as possible. "I want you to rest as much as you can. Both of us need to go away for a little while."

"Go away? You think I'm still in danger from that man?" She looked up at me, and the warmth of her body pulled away.

"No, not from that man. Just trust me. I want to keep you safe."

Raisa stared at me, her eyes unfocused. "You're going to take me away?"

"Yes. To a place where no one can hurt you."

"Oh, where no one can hurt me," she mumbled, burying her face into the crook of my neck and breathing against my skin. She fell asleep. Something felt wrong with her dazed responses. I held still, idly stroking the crown of her head. Surely the attack had not completely extinguished the inquisitive spark that endeared her to me so. Something else had made her dull and pliant.

I untangled myself from Raisa's arms and stepped into the kitchen. Mother sat at the table, resting her head against the back of her chair. Anyone else would have thought that she was sleeping, but I knew that she was alert behind her closed eyelids. A pot of tea already boiled over the fire, and sweet-smelling smoke filled the room.

"What did you do to her?" I asked in a cold whisper.

"Nothing." She opened her eyes, staring at me too innocently.

Mother was a masterful liar, and I could seldom tell when she was spinning a falsehood, but this time I was sure. "You've drugged her, haven't you?"

She tossed her curls over her shoulder as she rose from the chair, drawing herself up to her full height. I did the same. I had been as tall as she was for the past several years, and that trick would not work on me anymore. "It's for her own good, Ailynn. I thought about what you said to me, and you were right. A girl hidden away in a cave would go mad. This will calm her."

"But you've taken her will away!"

"I'm doing it because I love her," she protested, reaching out to touch my shoulder.

I shrugged her hand off. "You're insane."

"Cautious, not insane. It might seem cruel, but it's what's best for her."

"Then why not lock me away?" I spat. "Would that be best for me, too?"

"Of course I won't lock you away, you foolish girl. You can defend yourself, but Raisa…"

"I can protect her."

Mother left the table, turning her back to me as she walked over to the boiling kettle over the fire. She removed it and set it aside to cool, reaching up into the cabinet for two small cups. "Perhaps you are strong enough to defend yourself, but you're inexperienced, not to mention weak in matters of the heart. You are letting your feelings cloud your judgment."

"My feelings?" Something about the words sent threads of ice crawling beneath my skin.

She remained facing the counter as she prepared the tea, refusing to look at me. "You shouldn't underestimate my powers of observation, daughter. You are of my blood. I know how you think. How you feel."

My anger began to drain out of me, leaving only panicked confusion. "I don't understand."

"Either you are a better liar than I thought, or you are still naïve," Mother said. She turned around at last, holding a steaming cup in each of her hands. She motioned me over to the table, and something made me obey the gesture. I sank down into my chair while she studied me. "Or perhaps you simply haven't realized it yet."

"Realized what?"

"That you are in love with her."

The words struck me like a physical blow. I winced with pain and shame, realizing the truth in her words. I did love Raisa. I had sworn to care for her since the first night she spent in our home. I loved the joy she brought into any room she entered. I loved the way her imagination created stories and pictures out of simple, everyday things. I loved her innocence and kindness. "But I...she's—" I stammered, shaking my head.

Mother set one of the cups in front of me. "Only fifteen? Almost a sister? Take your pick."

"I'm not," I said, leaning back into the chair. "I'm not."

"If you're not, then why are you crying?"

I reached up to touch my cheek with my fingertips and felt hot tears clinging to my face. They seared into my flesh, more painful than fire. "No," I mouthed, but my voice was completely gone.

"Darling, beautiful girl, come here," Mother cooed, drawing my face against her stomach. I did not protest as she rocked me, and her hands rubbed along my back as I shook with sobs. "It's all right. She isn't really your sister, and she will grow. She is going to be a beauty in a few years, more than she is already. She is yours if you want her."

"You're doing it again," I cried, the words cracking in my throat. "You're treating her like a present that you can give to me."

"I did give her to you. I took her from her parents for you, remember?"

"I wish you had never brought her here. None of this would have happened."

Mother was silent for several beats. Finally, she spoke, but her words did not seem to be directed to me. "You truly do love her, Ailynn. You love her enough to give her up for her own happiness."

I pulled back, wiping the rest of my tears away with my sleeve. I folded my hands around the teacup and took a long drink, hoping it would soothe the painful sting in my throat. It did help. I sighed as I set it back down on the table. "I want her to be happy, and I know that no one can find happiness alone under the ground."

"That's what the herbs I gave her were for. To keep her content."

I set my cup back down. "They make her dull. She isn't fully aware of what is going on around her. She talks and moves as if she's in a dream."

Mother nodded. "I won't keep her this way forever, only until she is used to her new surroundings. She probably wouldn't object to becoming your lover in a few years, you know. You are the only person she has ever known aside from me."

I shook my head. "I refuse to take advantage of her that way. I can wait until she's old enough to understand. Then, I'll offer myself to her. If she wants me, I'm hers. If she doesn't, I'll help her find whoever she wants instead."

"You are too kind," Mother said. "You could easily make her love you with all of the knowledge I have given you, but you won't do it, not even for your own happiness. You would be good for her, Ailynn."

I glared at her. "Drugging her to win her love goes against my principles. I thought it went against yours as well."

Mother sighed and rested her hand on my shoulder. I was too muddled and confused to shove her away. "Love has made you weak. Someday, you will thank me for protecting her so well. Think, Ailynn. Raisa will never know pain beyond what she has already seen. She will be completely unspoiled by the world. Pure, trusting, innocent...everything that the girls in the village aren't. Protection is the greatest gift I can give to either of you."

"You've gone mad," I said, turning away from her. The motion made my head feel heavy, and I blinked to clear the lingering tears from my eyes.

"You should rest, daughter," she murmured. "Raisa might wake again."

It took my lips a few tries to form words. "I'm shocked she is still asleep after all the shouting."

"She needs her rest," Mother said. She took my cup away from me before I was finished, and I didn't think to protest. "So do you, my beautiful princess. Now, go to bed."

Strangely, I was not angry with Mother anymore. I did not feel anything except a heavy sluggishness settling over me like a thick blanket. "No." I tried to pick myself up out of the chair, but the weight of her hand made it impossible to move. "I need to...need...Raisa."

"Sleep well, daughter," Mother whispered beside my ear. "And don't feel guilty over this. I didn't teach you everything I know."

I slumped back into my chair and knew no more.

Rae D. Magdon

CHAPTER SIX

WHEN I WOKE THE next morning, I found myself in the bedroom instead of the kitchen. Raisa was not resting in my arms. Instead, a pile of rumpled sheets and a warm indent in the mattress remained in her place. My hands groped forward, trying to find her, but slowly, I began to realize that she wasn't there. She wasn't coming back.

After a few minutes of staring at the place where she should have been, my foggy brain finally understood what had happened. Mother had drugged me and taken Raisa after I had fallen asleep. I could detect almost any poison or sleeping draught by taste, but Mother knew far more about herbs than I did. She had probably found some way to trick my senses.

I blinked my eyes, struggling to clear my head. I had to do something to stop this, but I was still too dazed to come up with a plan. But I did remember something, something that had been drilled into me since childhood: *'Even wormwort, one of the strongest herbs we use to cleanse the body, can only be taken in the smallest of doses before it kills you.'*

Wormwort. I would need a considerable amount of the drug to come back to myself quickly, but Raisa could not wait. I fell out of bed and staggered into the kitchen, struggling to keep my balance. I clutched the door frame and turned around. "Herb room, please." It took a few tries for my thick, swollen tongue to form the words, but the door understood. The bedroom faded away, and the herb room came into view.

My hands fumbled across the shelves, knocking over several jars and baskets before I finally found the one I wanted: wormwort, right near the front so Mother could get to it easily. I snatched it up. It had already been crushed into powder, and I did not bother dissolving it further. I threw a pinch into my mouth and choked it down dry, shoving the rest of the jar away before I could tempt myself with more. The larger the dose, the quicker I would recover, but if I misjudged...

I stumbled back out into the kitchen and slumped down at the table. After a few minutes, my head began to clear. My limbs still felt unnaturally heavy, but my mind responded faster than before. I picked myself up out of the chair and hurried toward the door, grabbing a shawl to wrap around my shoulders as I slipped out into the sunlight.

By the time I arrived at the mouth of the cave, I knew it was too late. The edge of Raisa's braid lay coiled just outside the entrance to the tunnel. "Raisa?" I called, forcing my words out past the hard lump in my throat. "Raisa, are you in here?" There was no answer. The cave remained eerily silent. I summoned fire to light my way, following the golden thread down into the darkness.

With Raisa's braid to guide me, finding my way was easy. Other passageways branched off in every direction, but I ignored them, completely focused on my goal. As soon as I reached the cavern, I found the door open. Raisa was waiting for me. "Ailynn?" Her voice seemed small and frightened, but she smiled when she saw me and rose from the bed. "You came."

I took her into my arms, holding her tight against me. Her hands came up to clutch at my shoulders, and the tight ball of grief in my chest finally unraveled. I buried my face in her hair, hiding my tears.

"Oh, Raisa, I'm so sorry. I tried to stop her." I had been such a fool. Mother had already made it very clear what she was capable of when she had drugged Raisa, and yet I had fallen for the same trick. I had been arrogant, thinking my knowledge of herbs would protect me.

"This isn't your fault," Raisa said. "I remember some of last night. You said you wanted to take me away."

"That hasn't changed," I said, trying to steady my voice. No matter how horrible I felt, I could not let Raisa know how frightened I was. She had brought hope and love into my life since the day she came to me, and now, it was my turn to support her. "Come on. We have to leave. Has she left you anything sharp? We need to cut your hair."

Raisa sighed. "I already looked when I woke up. There isn't anything useful. She probably doesn't want me killing myself after I go crazy down here. But she isn't as creative as I am. I can see a dozen different ways."

Her words startled me so much that I let go of her arm and drew back in surprise. I had never dreamed that the bright, beautiful girl I had grown up with would mention suicide. "Please," I whispered, "don't say that. I wouldn't be able to bear it if you killed yourself."

Raisa's eyes narrowed. "All right. We don't have anything sharp." She turned around, lifting her braid away from her back and offering it to me. "So burn it off. This is the only guide we have."

My fingers clenched into fists. I had been wary of using my fire ever since I had killed the man in the clearing, and the thought of using it on Raisa was even more frightening. As wrong as she was about everything else, Mother had been right to say I lacked control.

Raisa must have sensed my hesitation, because she turned back around and stared at me over her shoulder. "Come on, Ailynn. We don't know when Mother Gothel's coming back. You have been playing with fire and cutting my hair for years. You can't tell me you've never thought of doing both at the same time."

I sighed. "Hold still. I don't want to burn you." I held up my hand and steadied it through sheer force of will. Even though I did not need to use Words of Power to conjure the elements anymore, I spoke it anyway, hoping it would give me the precision I needed.

"Fel."

Fire bloomed around my fingers, licking my flesh with a sweet, familiar pain. I sliced through Raisa's braid with one quick movement, cutting it just below the knot at the base of her head. The scent of burning hair made me wrinkle my nose, but I ignored it and concentrated. Just as I could give fire life, I could take that life away. I cut off the stream of energy I was feeding into the flames and choked them before they could drink from the air and grow.

Raisa's braid fell to the floor, and she tossed her head, exploring her new range of movement. "See?" She turned back around, staring down at the coiled, golden rope between our feet. "I knew you could do it. Let's get out of here before we lose our chance."

Together, we hurried to the exit. "You first," I said, giving her a gentle push in the middle of her back. "I'll light the way."

Raisa nodded, but when she tried to step across the threshold, her body froze. Her jaw bunched with frustration, and her arms trembled. "I can't," she said, still fighting against the invisible force. "Something won't let me cross. It's like there's a rope around my middle that I can't see. It's pulling me back." She threw her arms forward, reaching as far as she could, but even though they stretched into the darkness, the rest of her would not follow.

My heart sank. I knew exactly what the problem was, although that did not make it any easier to believe. "I have no idea how she did it, but Mother enchanted the room. She's bound you here."

"What?" Raisa stepped back from the doorway and looked at me in shock. "Mother Gothel's a Witch. She's not an Enchanter. Even I know that *Ariada* can only practice one type of magic at a time. She couldn't have."

"Not always," I murmured. "Lyr the Shaper and some of the High *Ariada* at Kalmarin learned other disciplines. I suppose it's not outside the realm of possibility that Mother could be expanding her knowledge."

Raisa lowered her gaze. "I thought those were just embellishments to make the stories better. You know how Amendyr's history is. Half of it's made up, and the other half is so crazy no one who lived elsewhere would believe it anyway." Her voice rose in pitch, and I could sense her panic growing.

I reached out and gripped her shoulders, forcing her to look at me. "If Mother learned how to bind you, I can learn how to un-bind you. I'll find a way to break the spell."

Raisa gave a slow nod, although she refused to meet my gaze. "I can help. Bring me any books you think would be useful from Mother Gothel's library. It looks like I'm going to have a lot of time on my hands anyway." She sniffed and swiped at her eyes with the sleeve of her dress. "You know, Reagan and Sawyea was always my favorite story, but I never thought I'd be playing both characters."

I reached out to cup her cheek. "They both went free in the end," I reminded her. "So will we. I'm not going to leave you here."

"That's what Saweya told Reagan," Raisa said. Her lips twitched up into a smile, and some brightness returned to her face. "You promise you'll get me out of here?"

I nodded. For Raisa, I would do anything.

* * *

Mother was sitting at the kitchen table when I returned to the cottage. She looked up when I stepped through the back door, watching me as I hung my shawl. I refused to look at her until she spoke. "Where were you, Ailynn?"

"Visiting Raisa," I said. The last thing I wanted to do was speak with her. Hate rose in me again, and I needed to get away from her before it surfaced. I walked over to the magic door and straightened my shoulders. "Library, please."

"I know what you're looking for in there," Mother said. "You shouldn't waste your time searching."

I tried not to answer her, but my anger forced me to. "If you don't want me to read your books, maybe you should drug me again. That seemed to work well enough last night."

"Ailynn." Mother stood up and reached out for me, but I did not allow her to finish. As soon as the door swung open, I stepped forward into the library and sealed myself inside, relieved to be away from her.

Like the treasure room, the library was completely disorganized. Books on history and affairs of state sat crowded next to bestiaries and recipe lists. Volumes that did not occupy the vast number of shelves lining the walls were stacked on tables and chairs instead, or spread haphazardly throughout the room. None of the furniture matched, and candle stubs littered the floor.

I settled myself down in an overstuffed, faded blue chair and grabbed the nearest spell volume, flipping through the pages as quickly as I could. Somewhere in the middle of the book, I found the edges of two torn pages near the binding. They had been deliberately ripped out. Refusing to let myself grow angry, I picked up the next book in the pile.

After several minutes of searching, I found three more references to the binding spell, but in each book, the pages I needed were gone. Mother's actions did not surprise me. Her paranoia had probably driven her to destroy all the pages about the spell. I was not overly disheartened, however. There were hundreds of books in the library. Surely she had missed at least one copy.

"I told you not to waste your time."

I closed the heavy book on my lap and looked up to see Mother standing in the doorway. "It isn't a waste of time if I free her," I said. "How did you do it, Mother? Did you spend the past few months learning how to become an Enchanter in secret, or did you hire someone else to do it for you?"

"You know the answer, Ailynn. I never pay anyone for work I can do myself."

"Raisa reminded me of something today. In the stories, whenever an *Ariada* twists nature to learn magic other than the type they were born with, the extra power always corrupts them. They become evil. What are you going to do next? Become a Necromancer or a Shaper?"

Mother narrowed her eyes. "If you think I'm so evil, why are you trying to do the same? You're no Enchanter. But even if you were, I made sure to erase the spell I used. This obsession of yours will fade, and after a while, you will realize that everything I did is for the best."

I stared at her, shock coiling through me. For all her faults, part of me still could not believe she did not show any guilt or remorse for what she had done. "If you still think this is for the best, why did you take all the sharp objects away from the cave? Raisa mentioned killing herself today."

For the briefest of moments, Mother's face cracked. Her eyes flashed with pain. Calling her evil had not worked, but if the thought of Raisa killing herself had upset her, perhaps she was not entirely gone. I set my book aside and stood up from the chair. "It was only in passing, but how do you think her mind will hold up after another month? A year? Please, Mother. You can end this. Just let her go."

Mother remained silent for a long time, but in the end, she turned away from me and shook her head. "I am sorry, Ailynn. I'm going to protect you both, even if it makes you hate me. Someday, you will understand."

CHAPTER SEVEN

I WOKE UP IN the library the next morning, unable to remember falling asleep. An open book rested in my lap, and sunlight streamed into my eyes from one of the windows. I squinted and uncurled myself from the seat of the chair, stretching my arms and yawning. The book fell to the floor with a thud. I did not bother to pick it up.

"This is going to take an eternity," I muttered, staring up at the library shelves. I had spent all of last night and a good part of the early morning searching for a copy of the binding spell, but my efforts had been in vain.

I selected a short stack of four volumes from the arm of the faded blue chair and headed for the door. Before I left, I grabbed a well-loved volume of fairytales off of a table and placed it at the top of the stack. Perhaps having one of her favorite books to read during our search might improve Raisa's spirits.

The kitchen was empty when I left the library. I started to turn for the back door, but changed my mind and made a quick stop in the herb room first. The jar of powdered wormwort root was still there, and I balanced it on top of the books. If Mother decided to drug Raisa again to keep her from harming herself, she would have an antidote on hand.

The bright colors of the leaves outside were fading, leaving most of the trees bare. Winter would come soon. Raisa's favorite time of year was almost over. The thought brought a wave of sadness with it, and I quickly shook my head to dismiss the feeling. However, some of it lingered even as I approached the mouth of the cave. Raisa's braid was still there, but the color was not quite as lustrous as I remembered. I followed where it led, and although the way was different, it did not take me long to find her room.

Raisa greeted me with a sad smile. "Are those for me?" she asked, looking at the books. I nodded and handed them over. "Oh, Ailynn, you brought my favorite," she said as she scanned the titles. She rushed into my arms for a hug, and I kissed her forehead, so glad to see her that I didn't even mind having the books between us.

"I thought you would enjoy them. I have something else for you, too. Did Mother bring you anything to drink?"

"There's fresh water inside," she said, leading me further into the cavern. It was not as I remembered it. Mother must have visited sometime while I was in the library, because the room was now full of beautiful, useless bobbles from the treasure room. Dresses, tapestries, golden jewelry, and even a plush bed for Sing. He lay curled at the foot of the canopied bed, and his eyes cracked open when he heard our footsteps. I wondered how he had managed to find his way through the twisting maze of the cave, but decided not to question it. "She thought I would like them," Raisa said, staring sadly at the treasures. She set the books down on a nearby writing desk. "I tried to tell her that the only thing I wanted was to leave, but she didn't listen."

I put my hand on her shoulder. "It's not your fault. She didn't listen to me, either. I think something is wrong with her mind."

She rolled her eyes. "You think so? Well, come on. I'll show you the water."

Raisa led me to a corner of the room where there was a fountain of clean water and a golden chalice. I took the dipper and ladled out some of the enchanted water, tossing a pinch of the powdered wormwort root into the chalice before passing it over to Raisa. "Here, drink this. It will stop mother from drugging you."

"I thought she might. She left food for me too, but I didn't eat it. Fool me once..."

I sighed. "I am more of a fool than you are. I should have seen it coming. The water is safe now, though. The wormwort will keep your mind clear."

"Good." She lifted the chalice to her lips and took a long drink while I set the wormwort on top of the vanity.

"You need to promise me you will only take it in small doses," I insisted. "Too much at once, and you could die. I haven't forgotten what you said yesterday."

Raisa lowered the chalice. "I am not going to kill myself, Ailynn. I have only been up here a day. There is still hope. What about those other books you brought? Did you find anything useful?"

I shrugged. "I haven't looked through them yet. I thought you might want to help. So far, all I've found are torn pages, smudged ink, and a spell to make your hair grow thicker."

That made Raisa smile. "That's the last thing I need, although maybe you could take a turn growing yours out for a change. Come on, let's start reading. Perhaps we can find something useful."

* * *

Time passed quickly in the forest. Weeks became months before I realized that they had slipped away. I was no closer to freeing Raisa from her prison, but the two of us settled into a bearable, if not happy, routine. Every day, I brought a fresh stack of books to the cave and spent as much time as I could with her. We poured through them, but always wound up disappointed.

Still, my reading did teach me a few things. I began to sense the enchantment Mother had used whenever I approached Raisa's prison. It trickled over my skin like warm rivulets of water, trailing over my arms and belly and giving me gooseflesh. It was different, and yet similar to the way my body felt when I used Words of Power. There was magic behind the enchantment, but it was written in a language I could not understand.

One day, frustrated by my lack of progress, I decided to abandon my books and examine the framework of the magic itself—the woven aura of power that surrounded the cavern like a net. This was called shape-magic. using the senses to 'see' the energy that made up a spell. Relying on the knowledge I had gained from my advanced reading, I could almost see white tendrils of magical energy forming a chain from Raisa to... where? After hours of pacing and examining, which Raisa bore willingly because of the hope that she might be freed, I was no closer to discovering the root of the enchantment.

I was severely disheartened, but Raisa reassured me. "I know you will find a way to free me, Ailynn. I believe in you."

Mother, however, was less than pleased with me. Ever since she had imprisoned Raisa in the cave, a great rift had grown between us. No longer did she call me her beautiful princess. Whenever she gave her approval for a successfully brewed potion or newly acquired skill, the praise rang hollow in my ears. Perhaps that was more my fault than hers, but it still hurt to have one of the only two connections nurtured during my life begin to unravel.

Reasoning with Mother was impossible. Raisa was the jewel in her crown, the prize of her collection, and she wanted me to have her. Perhaps she did it because she loved me. Perhaps she did it because being able to provide me with what I wanted most of all gave her a feeling of power over me. Maybe it was both. But I needed to free Raisa, even if it destroyed what was left of our relationship. My heart, not to mention my conscience, would not settle for anything less.

* * *

"Where were you?" I asked.

Mother, who had been trying to sneak in quietly through the back door, set her sack down on the floor and looked up at me. I was waiting in one of the wooden kitchen chairs, a book open on my lap. She rolled her eyes when she saw the title. "I told you to stop looking for a way to break the enchantment," she said, half-scolding and half-annoyed. "It has been almost a year. I expected better of you."

"And I expect nothing of you," I said, setting the book on the table. "Where were you last night?"

To her credit, Mother did not try to fabricate one of her usual lies. She knew I was far too old to believe them. Instead, she bent down and reached for the large, lumpy sack she had discarded moments before. I was faster. I scooped it up from the ground before she could get her hands on it and dumped out the contents. Several books fell onto the table, and I studied the titles curiously. "*The Art of Transmogrification. Lyr: A Biography. A History of Magical Creatures and Their Creators.* What kinds of books are these, Mother?"

"More books for the library," she said. "You have read everything else in there. I might as well give you something new to look through." I knew that there was more to tell, but did not push her. Mother had stopped telling me the truth a long time ago. "Ailynn, I have been thinking about you recently. You are a grown woman now. It is time for you take on more responsibilities here."

Although I still helped Mother whenever she prepared magical cures for the men and women that came to our house, I had been neglecting my duties lately. Brewing potions and making charms did not hold my interest like it used to. I had poured all of my energy into freeing Raisa from the cave, although I had little to show for it. "What kind of responsibilities?"

"I have decided to leave my practice to you. You are knowledgeable enough and skilled enough to take over for me. I have other projects I want to pursue."

I resisted the temptation to ask her exactly what these were. Perhaps they were part of the reason she had been disappearing lately. I just hoped it had nothing to do with the books I had seen. Enchanting was dangerous enough, but Shapers were even worse.

I arched my eyebrow. "Are you sure about this? Do you really think I'm ready, or do you simply want to make me forget about Raisa?"

"I know you, daughter. Nothing I say will convince you to stop trying to free her. I am not sure whether such devotion is admirable or foolish, but either way, you cannot spend your entire life obsessing over her."

I glared at her. "Why not? You have."

Mother simply glared back. "That is not the same thing, and you know it. But in the meantime, you might as well do something useful with your life. I expect you to take care of all the villagers who come here looking for your help. Spend your nights with Raisa, if you must. Between you and Sing, she will not be deprived of company."

And so I reluctantly took over Mother's business, which kept me occupied during most mornings and afternoons, but allowed me to spend the evenings and nights with Raisa. Despite the new workload, I did not give up my search for the binding spell. I sacrificed hours of sleep to go through the books in the library, often more than once. The results were always the same—pages referencing the spell were torn out and destroyed.

Raisa became more and more impatient as the months passed, but she rarely took out her frustrations on me. She knew I was trying to help her as best I could. She refused to allow her mind or body to become weak, and although being a prisoner often made her depressed, she fought her feelings of helplessness and frustration so that they would not overwhelm her. I doubted I would have been able to bear her burden with half the same grace.

Before I knew it, Raisa was sixteen years old, and I found myself admiring her body as well as her strength and perseverance. These feelings made me extremely uncomfortable. I was an academic and a loner, both by circumstance and by choice, and knew next to nothing about romantic entanglements. Although I had started puberty at twelve, my sexual development was delayed, to put it kindly.

Other girls my age were already taking lovers, even marrying and starting families, but I did not pay much attention. At twenty, I was almost an old maid by the standards of some. I researched the subject—Mother had some books on non-magical topics—and was surprised to discover that most other girls felt these strange stirrings much, much earlier than me.

Although I had been in love with Raisa for as long as I could remember, my daydreams had mostly been ambiguous, innocent ones about marrying her, starting a family, and living happily ever after as *Tuathe*. In my own personal fairytale, sexuality had never played a major role. But things began to change, and I was not sure if I liked it. I started having dreams, waking and sleeping ones, about what it would be like to kiss her. The more her body matured, the more involved these dreams became to the point where they embarrassed me. Just kissing no longer seemed like enough. I wanted more. I wanted everything.

The blossoming feelings of love and desire I was experiencing came with a price: frustration and guilt. I knew many women Raisa's age took lovers or married older men, but I still considered her far too young to be exposed to such things. It was difficult for me to stop seeing her as a child I needed to protect and start seeing her as a woman, although my body had certainly noticed and responded to the change without my permission.

I could be patient, I told myself. I could wait until I had freed her, until she had finished growing up. But when I woke in the middle of the night with my hand trapped between my legs, my fingers slick with wetness and my body covered in sweat, it was difficult to push down the desire I felt. I learned to take care of my need myself, but the end was never satisfying, and it always returned twice as strong every time I saw her.

CHAPTER EIGHT

MOTHER'S DETERIORATION CONTINUED. IT was as though locking Raisa away had only been the first step, and continuing down the wrong path became easier and easier with every stride. She hardly stayed in the house anymore. Dark bruises hung in half-circles under her eyes and lines covered her once-beautiful face. Her body also deteriorated, and her shoulders slumped further with each passing day.

I tried not to think about it, tried not to notice, because despite everything that had happened, a small part of me still loved her and missed the relationship we had once shared. Once, I followed her on one of her late-night journeys, determined to discover where she went and talk some sense into her. I wrapped my cloak around my shoulders, bolting all of the doors and windows behind me on the way out. Despite her constant paranoia, Mother was too distracted to pay attention to that sort of thing anymore.

She started off, not following any of the usual paths, but I knew the forest like the palm of my hand. As I trailed a short distance behind her, I began to notice a change in her. Her steps did not slow, but her gait became more shuffling and less forceful. Her back began to bend, and once I thought I saw white hair whipping around a tree instead of her glossy brown curls. Had she cast an illusion over herself to change her appearance? It was one more question to add to the long list already in my mind.

After we had walked a good distance, we came to a part of the forest I had not often explored. It was a place few travelers visited, and I suspected that was why Mother had chosen it. She valued her privacy. As I crept closer, I confirmed the presence of an enchantment surrounding her. Instead of standing straight and tall, she was curled over like a dying fall leaf, and her skin wrinkled and thinned. Her hair was white as snowdrop petals. She looked like a harmless old woman, and had I not seen the change myself, I would not have been able to recognize her. Her powers of enchantment had grown well beyond binding people to objects.

After a quick glance over her shoulder, she hurried past a curtain of leaves and disappeared. Worried I would lose her, I followed as fast as I could without drawing attention to myself, carefully picking my way over twigs and crackling leaves. When I reached the place where she had vanished, I could not see where she had gone at first. It took a few moments of careful inspection before I realized she had not gone forward, but down. Below me, covered by a carefully woven mat of greenery, was the entrance to a cave. As I peeled the mat backwards, the smell of damp limestone rose from below. It was familiar, and I suspected it was another entrance to the network of tunnels where she had imprisoned Raisa.

A high, keening howl jerked me upright, sending a shiver shooting up my spine. I was not afraid of wolves. They were not aggressive unless you invaded their territory or tried to take their kills. But something about the voice of that wolf, the voice of the forest, warned me of danger.

I sighed, chiding myself for my unfounded fears. "You are not a child anymore, Ailynn," I mouthed, careful not to speak aloud just in case my mother decided to come back out of the cave. But I could not shrug off the feeling of foreboding seeping into my lungs. Following my instincts, I turned back and returned to the cottage. I could not go further while Mother was still down there, and I did not want to get caught. I would come back later when I knew the cave was empty and conduct a proper search then.

* * *

Raisa's seventeenth birthday came, and I had no idea what sort of present to give her. Mother gathered several pretty trinkets to bestow on her, but I was not taken with any of them, and I knew that she would not be, either. The best present I could have given Raisa was certainly her freedom, but the two of us had searched Mother's library from top to bottom with no success. An awareness had also grown in me, a realization I did not want to face because it meant leaving behind what I cared about most in the world. I knew I would have to go out into the world and search for the spell I needed. I stalled as long as I could, unwilling to leave Raisa alone with Mother, but I knew that the time was coming for me to leave.

One of my reasons for waiting was also selfish. I also did not want to leave the woman I loved. And she was a woman now, as much as it frightened me to admit it. Her hair was healthy and strong, the color of golden summer wheat. It required a great deal of care, but the results were magnificent. Her body had softened and curved, narrowing at the waist and flaring at the hips. The softness of childhood had melted from her face, giving her a thinner, more adult appearance and wiser eyes.

Inspiration struck me as I walked to the cave. I knew what Raisa longed for most was to visit the world outside her prison. She missed the sights, the sounds, and the smells of the forest. I could not remove her from the cave, but perhaps I could bring a bit of the outside world to her. I hurried back to the cottage for supplies, grateful I was only a few minutes into my walk, and went out into my mother's garden.

I quickly found what I was looking for, a small patch of soft white flower buds. They were moonflowers, a relative of deadly nightshade and a staple in any apothecary's garden. They only unfurled their petals at night, and their blossoms would welcome the darkness of the cave. I took a trowel and a clay pot from the garden shed and set about my work, carefully excavating the tangle of roots.

As I moved the blossoms into the pot, I wondered if Mother would be angry with me for disturbing the plants in her garden. I dismissed those thoughts. This garden was as much mine now as hers, anyway, since I was the one who used it to help the villagers when they came to me with their problems. Soon, the job was done. I patted the dirt around the flowers so that it would not shake loose, brushed my hands clean on my working skirt, and straightened up with the pot in my hands.

The journey to see Raisa was always shorter when I approached cavern instead of leaving it. I must have been even more anxious to visit her on this particular day, because the journey seemed to take no time at all. Far sooner than I expected, I arrived at her room with my present in hand. I knocked on the door with my free hand. "Raisa? It's me. I have something special for you."

Raisa gasped when she opened the door and saw what I was carrying. "Oh, they're beautiful." She threw her arms around my neck, wrapping me in a tight hug. I smiled over her shoulder, proud of myself for coming up with a present that she liked and secretly enjoying the way that her curves melted into mine. I sighed, savoring the intimate contact. We fit together perfectly. "Thank you for my birthday present, Ailynn," she whispered, keeping hold of my hand.

Slowly, I forced myself to pull away and set the pot on the ground. Although I was deeply in love with her, I would never dream of making her uncomfortable. "I thought you would like them," I said, stumbling over my words. "I wanted to get you something beautiful, since I think you're beautiful. And I...I thought..."

Raisa laughed and pressed her finger to my lips. The simple touch made my skin burn, and a fierce blush crawled all the way up my face. "Shh," she whispered, leaning closer to me. "They're perfect."

And then she kissed me. It was a simple, soft meeting of lips that lingered for only a few seconds, but it nearly stopped my heart. We parted slowly instead, taking several moments to open our eyes and calm our racing hearts. I had suspected before, but now I was absolutely sure. Raisa was the other half of my soul, and I was lost to her for the rest of my life. We were *Tuathe*, two souls that are one.

I opened my mouth and tried to say her name, but I found myself falling into her again instead. The second kiss was deeper, longer, and the hunger I had restrained for the past year began rising to the surface. My hand clutched at her hip, drawing her body closer against mine. She leaned against me, and her fingers wove into my hair, holding us in place as her lips learned mine. By the time I finally broke away from her to breathe, my head spun. "Raisa? Are you sure this is what you want?"

She smiled at me. "Oh, Ailynn, kissing you didn't make it clear enough? Of course this is what I want. It's what I've always wanted. And I know it's what you want, too."

"I wasn't going to say anything," I mumbled. "I didn't want to assume."

Raisa stroked my cheek. "And that's exactly why I want this. You care what I think. You listen." Her eyelashes lowered flirtatiously, and my heart flew up into my throat. "And you didn't grow up to look half-bad, either."

Reluctantly, I let go of her hip and reached out to take her hand instead. "And you grew up to be the most beautiful woman I've ever seen."

"And just how many women have you seen?" she asked, narrowing her eyes.

"I'm not talking about looks," I whispered. "All of you is beautiful, Raisa. Inside and out."

Nothing else happened between us that night, but Raisa's hand did not let go of mine for the rest of the evening. We did not discuss the change between us, but I received a third magical kiss, just as sweet and innocent as the first, before I left her later that night. The last thing I remembered before I went to sleep was Raisa's beautiful face hovering close to mine, leaning for a kiss as the moonflowers unfurled their petals.

CHAPTER NINE

AS RAISA AND I explored the added depth to our relationship, Mother continued to grow restless. Although I was consumed by thoughts of love and happiness, I had not forgotten the secret cave I had discovered on the night I followed her. I thought of it often, and one day, my curiosity finally got the better of me.

I was walking back through the forest after a visit to Raisa when I nearly collided with another passerby, dodging to the right just in time to prevent an accident. "I'm sorry, did you need something?" I asked, wondering if a visitor seeking my help had found the cottage empty and gone searching for me. I peered at the person's face and started when I realized who it was.

Mother had taken the shape of an old crone again, but she did not seem to recognize me. Something else lingered in her expression, however. Something I could not name. It made my palms sweat and my heart batter against my ribs. She pulled her black cape tighter around her shoulders and hurried away from me without speaking, leaving behind the crackling scent of her magic. Threads of the spell drifted off of her like loose strands of hair brushed from a shoulder.

I stood there for several moments, confused by what I had seen. Why had Mother not recognized me or spoken to me? Could whatever magical experiments she was working on be eroding her mind? I tried to remember the last time she had acted normally, but I could not come up with a clear answer. My decision solidified. I needed to find out what she was doing in that cave. Something had poisoned her mind, and I had to find the cause.

I pulled my own cloak tighter around my shoulders and followed the path she had taken. She had traveled it so often that her feet had worn a thin impression into the ground. My feelings of unease grew stronger. The woman who had raised me would never have been so careless. It was further evidence of her deterioration.

I started to lose sight of her and fell into a jog, the sides of my skirt flapping behind me. The closer I drew to the secret entrance of several weeks ago, the quieter the forest became. I heard no birdcalls or rustling leaves, only the loud, crunching sound of my own footsteps on the forest floor.

I had never believed mere thoughts and actions could taint a particular place, but as I approached the woven mat covering the cave entrance, I began to doubt my assumptions. An essence of...something...swirled in the air. I recognized the taste and scent of raw power, but there was something else as well. Something dark, cold, and unpleasant.

Burying my feelings of foreboding, I gripped the edge of the mat in my hands and pulled it back. A puff of air came from inside the pit, rising up despite its cold temperature. For a moment, it seemed as though the cave itself was breathing. I released the breath I had not known I held, summoning a ball of flame and starting my descent.

As soon as I entered, I knew that this was the same network of tunnels that Mogra had used to imprison Raisa. The stone was the same texture, but infused with the subtle hum of magic. Since I had no braid to guide me, I took my best guess at the first fork, following the threads of enchantment I could feel woven into the walls. The deeper I travelled, the stronger the power became, until the smell burned in my nostrils. Soon, the cave rounded out into a basin-like chamber. To my surprise, shelves of books lined one of the walls. I hurried over to the first shelf. Perhaps the spell I needed to free Raisa was somewhere here. Had my mother been hiding it here all this time?

As I scanned the titles on the spines, some embossed in gold, some written with white chalk in my mother's familiar scrawl, I realized these books did not have what I was looking for. I recognized three of them: *The Art of Transmogrification, Lir: A Biography,* and *A History of Magical Creatures and Their Creators.* There were others, too: *Men from Clay* and *Beasts and Their Gods.* All of these books had one subject in common: the ancient practice of Shaping.

Shapers used magic to change, alter, or even create living beings. It was an old magic, very difficult to learn, and very powerful. Although some ancient Shapers had created the kind spirits of the forest and other good creatures, many of them created monsters. The Liarre, half-animal, half-human hybrids that lived past the western border, were the result of the Shaper Lyr's experimentations.

I turned away from the books to examine the rest of the chamber. A crowded square table stood in the middle of the room. Mixing bowls and measuring cups covered its surface. Ladles, knives, and other cutlery scattered between the bigger items. There were herb pouches, grinding pestles, and several lumpy packages I could not identify. Whatever Mogra was working on, she had certainly taken a long time to gather her materials.

Only after I had finished examining the table did I notice the other piece structure in the circular room. Tucked into a crevice, mostly hidden by shadow, was a square outline. I crept closer, the hovering ball of light guiding my way. In the darkness, something glinted. Cages! The other side of the room was lined with them. What could she be keeping there? I took another cautious step forward and peered at the rusted, twisting things made of dull metal. Although the bars had been chipped, none had been bent. They looked strong. Each cage had only three sides, with the cave wall making up the fourth. My stomach sank.

Although they were empty now, I could guess what Mother had been keeping in those cages. They were the perfect size for humans. But where were they now? What had they become? The weight of dread settled over my shoulders as I accepted what I had been denying. Mogra had gone completely insane.

The sound of footsteps echoing from the entrance of the cave startled me. I ducked underneath the table and extinguished the globe of light with a frantic whisper. The tiny sphere winked out like a dying star, leaving me in darkness. A soft humming began somewhere to my left. The wordless, keyless tune stretched into the empty space between us. I recognized the timbre of the voice, the silhouette I could just barely make out as a candle flared to life on the other side of the room.

"I see you, Ailynn," the old woman cooed, although she was not looking beneath the worktable. I shuddered, hardly recognizing her voice. "Stop hiding from me."

Praying my legs would continue to support my weight, I crawled out from under the table and stood to my full height. "Mother." She did not react. "Maman," I tried again, hoping that the informal childhood name would stir some feelings of love in her. There was no spark of recognition, no glint of warmth in her cold, metallic eyes.

"I will have to punish you for coming here," she said. Although her body seemed old, leathery and twisted like a knotted piece of sea rope, her voice came out clear and strong, the voice of a much younger woman.

"Oh, Mother," I murmured to myself. "What has happened to you?"

"I have been making things." She stared at the empty cages with frosted eyes, as though she had forgotten I was there. "Wonderful things. Terrible things. I have been making things for Her."

I swallowed, trying to ease the dryness in my throat. Nevertheless, my voice cracked as I asked, "Who?"

"Her," Mogra repeated. "She needed an army, and paid me well to build it for her."

"Mother, whatever Shaping magic you have been doing, it needs to stop. It's changing you." A terrifying thought flitted through my head, forcing itself to the forefront of my mind. Fear's frozen hand squeezed the warm blood from my heart. "Have you...done anything to Raisa?" Although I spoke in a whisper, the walls of the cave amplified the words to a shout.

"Raisa?" At first, she peered at me. Then her eyes cleared for a moment, and she almost smiled. "My treasure? No. Raisa must stay with me forever."

Forever, the ghostly, echoing voice of the cave whispered in my ear. *Forever.* Mogra would not try to harm Raisa. She did not think of her as a person anymore. She was just a pretty toy, an ornament to be admired. I could not decide whether to be frightened or relieved. In my mother's eyes, Raisa was not human, but at least she was not a potential experiment. Tears needled my eyes, threatening to spill over the brim of my cheeks and roll down my face. I could do little for Mother now. She had lost herself to whatever insane magical forces she had been experimenting with.

"Yes, Raisa is your treasure," I said soothingly, slowly backing towards the mouth of the cave. "I will go to Raisa now." Mother only stared at me as I retreated. For just a moment, I thought I saw her back straighten, and I caught a glimpse of auburn in her snow white hair.

"Stop." Mogra's young voice was layered with overtones, and it halted me before I could edge out of the cavern. "Who told you to come here? Did they send you?" She seemed to grow larger, her disguise flickering in and out. I saw glimpses of my mother's young face before

54

the torn patches of the spell repaired themselves. She was caught between two different shapes, unsure which she wanted to take.

We both moved in the same moment. I ducked back into the tunnel as Mogra lifted her hand, cradling a crackling ball of flame in her palm. It was much larger than my tiny globe of light had been, and its heat burned my flesh even from several yards away. Too startled and frightened to shield myself, I turned and bolted for the surface as fast as I could, stumbling up the steep slope of tunnel.

Fire roared behind me. I could feel it feeding on the air, exploding through the cave and threatening to devour me. If I ran, I would not be fast enough. I turned around, gritting my teeth as I braced my feet on the tunnel floor. My hands flew out, reaching for something to use, but there was nothing dry enough to kindle. Surrounded by cold, damp stone, I reached inside of myself instead, gritting my teeth against the pain as fire flew from my palms. My pain fed the blaze. Fire and its anger was mine to control. I would not let it destroy me.

My flame collided with hers. The two forces met, then exploded outward in a brilliant arc. Streaks of white and red raced along the tunnel wall, and I clamped my eyes shut against the light. Heat washed over my face. A crunching sound grated in my ears, and I realized the heat of the fire was splitting the stone around us. The cave began to tremble. This time, I clambered up the steep slope as fast as I could, bursting out into the fresh air.

The aftershocks came seconds behind me. A fresh wave of fire spat from the entrance to the cave, billowing up into the air. I stumbled back, clawing at the dirt, before its arms could reach me. A column of bright light seared against the sky, and I was certain it would swallow me whole. But the fire faded to sparks, and soon, the dazzling flare dissolved back into the night sky.

I pushed myself on to my feet and continued running, not stopping to see if Mogra had decided to come after me. I suspected she had stayed behind. Perhaps part of her still recognized me as her daughter. But I knew one thing for certain—it was too dangerous for me to stay in the forest any longer. I had to leave as quickly as I could.

Rae D. Magdon

CHAPTER TEN

I CRASHED THROUGH THE darkness, hurrying toward the other entrance to the cave where Raisa slept. Several times I feared I was running in the wrong direction, but my legs had traveled the path so often I did not even need to think. My lungs burned from smoke, and my wounded hands throbbed with their own heartbeat. I had to get away. Mogra had become too dangerous, too unpredictable to deal with. Although I had managed to escape this time, I might not be so lucky again.

A painful lance of guilt pierced my stomach, forcing me to slow my run to a jog. It was easier to think of my mother as Mogra now, easier to separate myself from her. My mother. The beautiful woman who had thrown me in the air so I could pretend to fly. The woman who had taught me which herbs restored health and which caused sickness. The woman who had given me fire. The woman who had given me Raisa. Had she always been this way? Had I simply refused to see it? Or had something twisted her beyond recognition?

Despite our estrangement after she locked Raisa away, I still cared for her. Even now, I could not help but love her in some small way. At least, I loved what she had once been. I had no love for the madwoman in the cave. She was not my mother. She was someone else, something else.

I stopped short as I came to the mouth of Raisa's cave. Her golden braid was tucked near the edge, and I followed the shining coil into the black pit below. I stumbled in my hurry, catching myself on the stone and hissing in pain as I scraped my raw hands. The sting made my eyes water, but I pushed it down. There would be time for a poultice later. I needed to make sure that Raisa was safe.

I navigated the tunnels as quickly as I could, but it still seemed to take years to reach Raisa's room. She was asleep when I entered, curled into a ball beneath the bedcovers. The only light came from the false stars above us and the glowing white petals of the moonflowers.

"Raisa," I whispered, keeping my voice soft. I could just make out her form beneath the sheets. The top of her long braid was coiled above her head like a great golden snake, piled in strange curved patterns over her pillows. "Raisa," I repeated, a little louder.

This time, her lashes fluttered. She stretched her arms and rubbed at her eyes with a tired hand. "Ailynn? Wha...why are you here?" she asked, her voice breaking with sleepiness.

"I'm sorry for waking you. I had to come see you."

"Something is wrong," she said. She groped for the matches on her bedside table, but I lit the candle first, touching my fingertips to the wick. After a moment, faint light filled our corner of the room. Raisa frowned when the candle's flame fell on my hands. "What happened? Tell me, Ailynn." I avoided her eyes. "I've never seen you burned so badly."

I tried to speak, to explain why I was there in the middle of the night, but I could not find the words. Her fingers reached out, clasping the backs of my hands. She did not dare touch my palms.

My jaw finally loosened. "She tried to kill me today," I said, forcing my voice past the tight ball in my throat. "She is completely insane now. I think she's conducting some kind of experiment in the secret cave she hides in."

"She attacked you?" Raisa pulled me down onto the mattress and began pushing aside my clothes to search for other bruises and cuts. "Did she hurt you anywhere else?" For once, her touch did not make my heart pound and my hands tremble. I could only remember that I was leaving.

"No, she didn't hurt me," I said, unable to meet her eyes. I stared at the headboard of her bed instead, following the patterns in the grain of the wood. The flickering candlelight gave the illusion of movement. "But I can't stay here. I have been through every book in the library twice. With moth...with Mogra like this, we need to escape more than ever. I have to find a way to free you."

Raisa's hands lingered for a moment, and then fell away. The loss of her touch left a gaping hole somewhere in the middle of my chest. Instead of looking surprised, she seemed resigned. "Then I'll wait for you," she promised, the edge of her leg just barely pressing against mine. She leaned closer, allowing our shoulders to brush as well. "I'll wait for you, as long as you promise to come back."

For a fraction of a second, I sensed her fear. I could not see it in her face, but it radiated from her body in one short, sharp pulse, so strong I could almost smell it. She was terrified I would leave her here. That I would forget about her.

I pulled her into my arms and held her as tight as I dared, not caring how much it hurt my hands or my heart. "I promise," I whispered against the crown of her head, placing a kiss on top of her golden hair. "It would be impossible for me to forget you." She whispered something, only a few words, but I could not make them out because her face was still buried in my shoulder. "What was that?"

"I love you," she murmured. A soft, hesitant kiss brushed against the dip in my throat where it ran into my shoulder. My heartbeat sped up, and my breath caught. "Stay with me tonight, Ailynn. Please. I won't be able to sleep without you."

"If you let me, I'll stay with you forever," I said in a shaking voice. Raisa began to draw away from me, but I gripped her tighter, unwilling to let her go. "I love you, too." This time, my voice came out stronger. I believed in those words with all my heart. Something wet seeped through the material of my dress. Raisa was crying. "No, please don't cry."

"They aren't all bad tears. Is it strange to say that this is one of the happiest and saddest nights of my life at the same time?" Raisa loosened our embrace enough to look up at me with glistening eyes. Before I could process the change, she cupped my face with gentle hands and brought our lips together.

I had kissed Raisa with joy before, with love, and even with restrained desire. But until that moment, I had never tasted sadness in another person's lips. When she pulled away, only an inch, I was not sure if the kiss had left my heart empty or full. It was not enough, so I kissed her again. She opened her mouth against mine and her hand curled around my hip.

Both of us knew we could not go any further. Not tonight. I wanted the memories to be beautiful, not the beginning of a painful goodbye. Without asking, I sensed Raisa felt the same. Neither of us slept much that night. We spent most of the long, dark hours crying, kissing, and listening to each other's breathing. Even while we held each other close, loneliness, love's companion, crept over me like a thick gray fog.

The next morning was dark, a reflection of my mood. The image of the sky above our heads was a sickly gray pallor. I had hardly slept at all during the night, but Raisa, at least, got a few hours of fitful sleep beside me. I was content to hold her, trying to memorize how she felt in my arms just in case I never got the chance again. Carefully peeling myself from her tight embrace, I crept out of bed. When her empty arms reached out for me, I eased a pillow into the empty space. It must have carried my scent, because she buried her face in the fabric and pulled it closer to her chest.

My insides tied themselves in slippery knots, and my guilt grew stronger. For several minutes, I could only stare at Raisa as she slept. Even though I knew Mogra would not allow me to stay, even though I knew I had to find a way to release Raisa from the enchantment keeping her prisoner, I felt like a coward. I had insisted again and again that I could protect her, but what kind of protector was I really, running away like a frightened child?

I forced myself to turn away from her, and the room's colors seemed to fade right before my eyes, washing back into dull browns and grays. I did not know how to say goodbye. Perhaps it would be easier to leave before she woke up. It would be less painful for both of us. Moving quietly over to her small writing desk, I searched for a piece of paper and an inkbottle. I chose a quill and ran the soft edge of the feather along my cheek, searching for the right words. Eventually, I gave up on finding the right words and began to write:

Raisa,

I love you. I have always loved you, and that love has only grown with you. Sometimes, the depth of this love frightens me. I have never felt anything so strongly before.

It seems that most of my memories are of waiting—waiting for you to grow up, waiting to tell you my feelings, waiting to free you so we can begin a life together. I would wait until the end of the world for you, but the time for waiting is done. You deserve to be free and reclaim the world for your own.

This separation will not be forever. Soon, we will walk away from this place hand in hand, just like Reagan and Sawyea. Please do not hate me for leaving you behind. I promise I will always come back to you. I can only pray you will still love and want me when I return.

Wait for me. Please. Even though I am unworthy of the gift of your love, I am asking for it anyway. Wait for me. I will find a way to free you, no matter how long it takes.

Forgive me.

I did not sign the bottom of the letter, too ashamed of myself to put my signature on it. Sick with the knowledge of what I was about to do, I carefully folded the paper and set it beside the guttering candle on her night table. Tears pricked my eyes, but I could not cry. I had to prepare. If I was going to leave and search for a way to free Raisa, someone else would have to bring her food. Perhaps I could hire someone from the nearby village to do it. I certainly had enough coin, thanks to Mother's business. I would go to town, purchase supplies for my trip, and make sure Raisa would be taken care of.

Before I left the cave, I stole one final look at Raisa's face. In sleep, she looked more peaceful than I had seen her in years. I could almost pretend she wouldn't miss me. I forced myself to turn away, smothering the flame with a quick wave of my hand and casting the cavern into darkness.

PART TWO

Taken from the verbal accounts of Ailynn Gothel, Recorded and summarized by Lady Eleanor Kingsclere, née Sandleford

Rae D. Magdon

CHAPTER ONE

ONE YEAR. TWELVE TORTUROUS, lonely months apart from my beloved. I do not like to think of that year. Like the seemingly endless plains of the Eastern Kingdom, the villages I stayed in and the people I interacted with blurred together. I missed Raisa terribly. A year of my life—our life together—was gone, and I grieved its passing. My memories of that time are gray, colorless recollections of little importance. They did impart one lesson to me, though, one I never forgot: living without Raisa was not really living at all. I existed, I breathed and moved and spoke, but my emotions were gone. I became a cracked, brittle shell of myself.

Alone for the first time, I sank into a deep depression. Only thoughts of returning to save Raisa kept me from complete despair. I refused to give up hope. I would find the spell I needed to free her. I became a wanderer, traveling beyond the edges of the forest and into the central part of the kingdom, seeking out everyone who studied magic. Someone, I knew, would be able to help me. I could not bear to think of the alternative.

But the Kingdom was changing around me. Whispers of black sorcery filled the air, of evil rising up from the darkness to consume the white-cliffed city of Kalmarin. A proclamation was issued, and even I, in my haze of pain and loneliness, took notice. Amendyr had a new Queen. The King had died under mysterious circumstances, and his second wife took over his duties to the crown. Strange things began to happen. Tales of weird, twisted creatures spread from village to village. Giant, demonic dogs with eyes of fire began attacking in the night. No one had ever seen their like before, but they quickly earned themselves a name—the shadowkin.

The shadowkin did not hunt alone. Sleek, brown creatures made from mud and dust and human ashes accompanied them. The kerak were much more ancient creatures, but just as deadly. They resembled humans, but their limbs stretched beyond reasonable proportion, and they could run on all fours. Their hands bore scythe-like claws, perfect for ripping flesh. They feared fire, and usually prowled near the outskirts of the villages as they burned, making sure no one escaped alive.

Talk of rebellion also drifted about. Everyone knew the Queen was behind the terrible massacres, although most did not dare to say so aloud. Wherever I went, I saw able-bodied men and women leaving their families behind to head for the Rengast Mountains. As I traveled the flat plains at the heart of the kingdom, fear's choking grip settled over my shoulders. Fear has a taste; a dry, bitter taste that clogs the throat and cuts off the breath.

Three times, fate chose the town I was passing through for its next cruel blow. The first time, I awoke to the unforgettable scent of burning flesh and the coppery smell of blood. My heart jerked in my chest and it took me a moment to remember to breathe. Once I had my terror under control, I went to the window to see what was happening. When I opened it, screams pierced my ears. The shouts and cries blended together into an inescapable wall of sound. I was beyond fear now. I was numb. It would only be a matter of time until the creatures got to the boarding house.

I crept down the stairs and out the back door as quietly as I could. The men in black armor did not see me as I slipped out onto the street, or if they did, they chose not to pursue me. Passing the kerak was harder, but they gave me a wide berth when they saw the magical flames licking at my hands. Although my heart screamed with guilt as I left the village behind, I reminded myself that I needed to stay alive—if not for my own sake, then for Raisa's.

The second time I encountered the Queen's forces, I had time to prepare. I was already leaving the village, and I saw them coming as I stood on a high hill. A large, dark block of them appeared against the horizon in the south. With hatred stinging in my eyes, I turned away and urged the horse I had bartered for into a run. I could do nothing else. Warning bells already rung from the towers, so there was no need for me to go back. I ran as fast and as far as I could, but not far enough to escape the flicker of burning houses in the distance.

Despite the increasing danger, I continued traveling. The going became rougher. People grew less hospitable, fearing anyone they did not know might be a spy for the Queen. I did not blame them. I stayed in the small villages and towns for no more than one night, only long enough to ask where the most knowledgeable magical person in the area was. Some of these people knew of the binding spell, but none could help me. Unfortunately, many powerful *Ariada* had already left to join the rebellion or gone into hiding. I began to consider changing course for the Rengast and seeking out the rebellion as well.

Only three weeks after I saw the Queen's forces marching across the downs from my hilltop perch, I encountered her forces a third time. I had been traveling quickly, hardly stopping since sleep usually left me more exhausted than staying awake. I recognized the scent first. The clawing, biting scent of blood and fear burned through my throat. I smelled it over the meat in my stew, and all thoughts of dinner were forgotten. I stood and prepared to run, barely pausing to grab my pouch of coins.

Heat blasted over me as soon as I opened the door. It seared my face and hands, and I pulled back, retreating to the farthest wall in my room. I could not see the fire yet, but I could sense it beneath me, tearing through the ground floor. There was no way to escape through the front door. I had to climb down. I hurried to unlatch the window, pushing it open and gasping for fresh air. It was not much better outside. Other houses burned, and the streets filled with screaming masses of people.

I put one foot over the windowsill and looked down, reeling with vertigo as I realized how far I would have to jump. I knew fire, and this blaze was already well beyond my control. Shaping it to my will would take time and strength I did not have. I swallowed, took a deep breath, and hopped over the edge, gripping the windowsill with my hands and hanging as far as I could before dropping to the ground.

I hit the hedge beneath the window with a rustling crash, but the chaos around me prevented anyone from noticing. A wave of dizziness made me clutch at the wall as I clambered to my feet. My shoulder throbbed, and my knees ached from the fall, but I gritted my teeth and pushed the pain to the back of my mind. The men in black armor had already swarmed into the town, swords and axes drawn. Some carried torches, but most of the buildings around me were already engulfed in flames.

But the Queen's men were not the only danger. I caught a glimpse of a giant, hulking shape further down the street, and I ran in the opposite direction. Soldiers I could handle, but the shadowkin? No, they were too large for me to fight on my own. I hurried back the way the invaders had come, picking my way past several bodies. Most of them rested in pools of blood. None moved. *There is nothing you can do for them*, I thought, but the tears that ran from my eyes had little to do with the smoke.

Just before I rounded the last corner, a gloved hand clamped tight over my mouth. I tried to speak a Word of Power, but the magic died on my tongue. "Ay," a scraping voice shouted, far too close to my ear. "I've got a fresh one."

My gaze veered wildly, and for a moment, I could only see blurred streaks of darkness. More men came. They surrounded me, closing in with naked blades, but one of them had a torch. I narrowed my eyes and pushed, feeding air into the blaze. It grew and sputtered, lashing back and forth in the soldier's hand.

"What?" he shouted, and it was enough to get the rest of the group's attention. I made the fire race along his arm, and he stumbled back, dropping the torch in surprise.

The grip on my mouth loosened, and this time, the Word of Power came spitting out of me, blistering my tongue. *"Fel!"* The flames around me became my shield. I called them from the burning houses, from the smoldering rubble on the ground, and drew them toward me in coiling ropes. They stretched up from my feet, reaching for the sky. The man that had been about to kill me darted away. I did not give him the chance to escape. The wall of fire swallowed him whole, and his cries of agony rose above the billowing smoke.

I turned and ran for the darkness at the edge of the village. If I could just get away from the worst of the fighting and slip out of sight, my fire would keep me safe. But the darkness did not protect me. As soon as I stepped beyond the last building, I was surrounded. Tall, lanky forms prowled out from the shadows, and when the flickering light from my hands hit their faces, I stumbled back, gripped with terror.

Kerak. I knew what they were, but I was not prepared for the horrible, twisted creatures that stood before me. They had no eyes or noses, only wide, gaping mouths. Their bodies were long and angular, and their knotted arms ended in hooks. One of them turned toward me, and a scream died in my chest as it pulled its lips back over three rows of black, dripping teeth.

I heated the flames around my fists until they burned a brilliant blue, too terrified to notice the pain. The kerak lurched back in fear, its spine hunching low between its shoulders, but it did not retreat. The others crouched on either side of me, lurking just out of reach, and I knew that only my fire held them at bay. This time, I did not need my Word of Power. I threw out my hand and pushed.

Fire flew from my fingertips, lashing at the dark shape of the kerak. As soon as the first sparks touched its skin, its entire body went up in flames. The fire raced along its flesh, devouring everything they touched. It howled as its face began to crumble, and I stepped back in shock. I had known that kerak were vulnerable to fire, but I had never seen anything burn so quickly.

The rest of the kerak shrieked, lunging forward as one. Alone, they could not hope to escape my magic, but they could overwhelm me with numbers. I whirled around just in time to see a wicked pair of hooks curving toward my face. I threw up my hands, and the flames licking along my arms proved enough. The kerak's arms dissolved into ash, and it fell to the ground. But I could not face everywhere at once. Pain exploded along my shoulder, and I screamed as curved black teeth tore at my flesh. Before I could summon more fire, I found myself staring into a gaping, endless mouth. My heart stopped, certain that mouth would swallow me whole.

Suddenly, a red-black gush spurted from the kerak's throat. It reeled back, crumpling to the ground with the life snapped out of its neck. The creature I saw standing before me when it fell was even more terrifying. She was tall, taller than any human I had seen, and covered in red fur. I could only tell her gender because of the high breasts just below the mane at her neck. My eyes locked on her huge mouth and the long, dagger-like teeth behind her lips. Just as frightening as the kerak's, the points were smeared with thick red-black blood.

The other kerak tried to turn and run back to the main group, but there was no main group anymore. The strange creature I faced had not come alone. There were others like her, at least two score, pouring into the village. Many carried torches, but some of them were using magic. The smell of it did little to cover the scent of smoke and death, but the humming energy comforted me. They were fighting the kerak, and the kerak were actually retreating into the gutted buildings, trying to find positions of defense. I was not going to die.

I looked back at the red beast, fighting against the darkness that swam around the edges of my vision. No, not a beast. A wolf. I had not recognized it before. Still, something overwhelmingly human hid in its green eyes. I was amazed when it—she—inclined her head. Frozen stiff, I did not move to respond. My vision began to blur, but a low moan startled me from my daze. The creature began to change. It was a strangely smooth process, like the blowing of melted glass. The last thing I remembered before darkness swallowed me whole was a fiery-haired woman and a pair of bright green eyes.

CHAPTER TWO

"WAKE UP, AILYNN."

A smile twitched at the corners of my lips as Raisa's golden voice spoke to me. Her hand touched my shoulder, tugging gently at my sleeve. "Raisa?" I murmured sleepily, turning toward the sound of the voice.

"Ailynn, wake up." She moved further away, as though calling to me from a great distance. "Wake up." I tried to lift my hand, but my arms and legs were coated in lead. I could not move. Once again, I tried to reach out to her. Firm fingers gripped my hand. "Wake up..."

I opened my eyes. A woman was staring down at me, but not Raisa. The tone of her skin and the color of her eyes were all wrong. My heart splintered, and tears welled up, pressing out against my eyelashes.

"I thought we had lost you, Ailynn. You are lucky to be alive." I tried to sit up, but the woman placed a gentle hand in the middle of my chest. "No, stay where you are." I obeyed. My head spun, and my shoulder and hands ached terribly. Despite my strange surroundings, my instincts told me I was not in danger anymore. The smell of fear and blood had faded, and all that remained was the clean smoke of cook fires.

Knowing better than to try and rise again, I remained still on the bedroll and stared up at the stranger. Her green eyes were familiar, as was the color of her wild red curls, but they did not cover her entire body. This time, I recognized her as my savior. "Who are you? What are you?"

"My name is Cate." Her accent sounded similar to mine, an unusual mix of Amendyrri and Serian. Either she had been born on the border like me, or she had lived in both countries. She gave me a friendly smile, but her eyes had dark half-circles under them. I wondered when she had slept last. "My mate, Larna, leads the Farseer Pack. We fight with the Rebellion."

My eyes widened. "You are a Wyr," I said, my cheeks heating up at the breathless wonder in my own voice. I had read enough bestiaries and magical texts in Mother's library to recognize a Wyr, but I had never imagined I would see one for myself.

"I am." Cate lifted the hem of her shirt to reveal a thin strip of fur around her hips. The magical wolf skin belt had allowed her to become the beast that had rescued me.

"I owe you my life. Thank you."

"You are welcome, Ailynn."

"That's the second time you've used my name. How do you know me?"

Cate's smile fell away. "It was no accident that I rescued you last night. The spirits showed you to me in another realm." There was power and magic in her voice, and the force of it made me gasp. "I am a Shaman, a daughter of the Seventh Daughter. I have Known of you for a long time."

I knew the history she was speaking of, the seven siblings that had begun the Amendyrri tradition of magic centuries ago. The Wizard, the Shaper, the Enchanter, the Oracle, the Druid, the Necromancer, and the Shaman: seven of the Blood called to spread high magic, for both good and evil purposes, throughout the entire world. "I am Ailynn, Daughter of the First Son. What do you Know of me?"

Cate pressed her lips together. On closer inspection, she had to be close to my age. She was only a young woman, and if I had not seen differently, I would not have believed she was both a Wyr and a Shaman. "I know more than your name, Ailynn Gothel. I know that you are seeking a spell, one that will free the woman who waits for your return. I can help you."

Those words shocked me more than anything else. My heart swelled with a fierce joy, and laughter bubbled up in my chest. "You have it? You can help me? What kind of spell is it? Where—"

"So many questions," Cate sighed. "Wait, stay on your back. I will show you what you want to see, but please hold still. I worked hard to fix you, and I don't want your bandages to come undone."

She moved away and, quivering with excitement, I tried to see what my host was doing without lifting my head or neck. It was no use, and I contented myself with listening as she moved about the tent. All sorts of thoughts ran through my head, but one stood out above the rest: I could return home and see Raisa again.

Cate sat down beside my bedroll, carrying a large, leather-bound book with her. "I have carried this with me for months. Its owner is a dear friend of mine, and she risked much to have it smuggled across the border from Seria. I knew that you would need it, and she gave it to me when I asked, despite how protective she and her wife are of their library. It is yours." She passed the book to me, and I almost dropped the heavy tome as I took it from her with trembling hands. "What you want starts on page one ninety-three."

I flipped through the yellowed pages so fast I almost tore them, but Cate did not complain. The spell was on page one ninety-three, just as she had said. My heart leapt into my throat as I read the curling script, *Of the Enchantments Theories Necessary to Bind a Person's Aura to a Place or an Object of Power*. No longer caring what the book said now I had the spell in my grasp, I set it aside and sat up despite Cate's protests. I threw my arms around her neck and squeezed her tight.

"Thank you," I whispered as tears ran down my cheeks. "Thank you so much."

"What is this?" a low, teasing voice called out from the open flap of the tent. "Do I see my mate in the arms of another woman?"

Startled, both of us pulled back. Cate adjusted the front of her tunic and turned to look at the newcomer. One of the warmest, loveliest smiles I had ever seen broke across her face as she stood to greet the dark-haired figure entering the tent. The woman was tall and broad-shouldered, and though she carried no weapons, I could tell at first sight she was a warrior. They melted in to each other, and Cate's face buried in the warmth of the other woman's neck. I must have been staring for a long moment, because both of them realized they were being watched.

"Ailynn," Cate murmured from within the circle of her lover's arms. "This is Larna, Alpha of the Farseer pack. She is my *Tuathe*."

"Arim dei," I said. Although the sight of a closely bonded pair like Larna and Cate would have made me sick with loneliness only a short time ago, the sight of them reminded me of the woman I would be returning to instead. After a year of grief, frustration, and fear, I had finally found what I was looking for. I smiled. "My name is Ailynn. I promise I was not trying to steal your wife."

73

Larna smiled at me over top of Cate's head, brushing a kiss over her bright red curls. "Of course not. I'm honored to meet you, but I think I will be staying over here all the same. Cate is hating it when anyone comes near her patients."

"You have her well trained, Cate," I joked, feeling so light that I thought I would float through the top of the tent and touch the moon. Both of them laughed, and soon I was laughing with them, tears spilling freely from my eyes. My shoulders heaved as I sobbed into the traveling blanket draped across my lap.

Cate hurried over to comfort me, and Larna followed after. I sensed rather than saw their movements because my vision was still blurry. *Soon, soon,* the voice in my head kept chanting. *Soon, you will be home. Home. Home with Raisa.* All of the emotions I had locked inside myself for over a year came spilling out, flooding me with so many sensations at once that I could not sort through them all. "I'm sorry," I said, my voice breaking. "I'm just...I'm so happy."

"It's all right," Cate whispered. She rubbed small circles on my back until my heaving sobs calmed to small hiccups. "I do not know all of your story, Ailynn, but I hope you will tell it to me someday. For now, I am glad you are happy. You do not have to explain anything."

I smiled at her, too grateful for words. Not only had she saved my life, she had given me back my soul.

* * *

I stayed with the rebellion for several days as I regained my strength. There were almost a hundred warriors in our group, both human and Wyr, and I learned this was only one small part of their force. I had not suspected the rebellion was already so large and well organized, but it was pleasant news to receive.

Larna was obviously one of the leaders. Although young, Cate explained to me that she was the Alpha of all the Wyr in camp, and there were several. I could always tell which of the humans around me were Wyr. There was a quickness in their movements, a primitive aura surrounding them. They were marching west, trying to cut off the Queen's probing forces. When they could, they stopped her soldiers and creatures, but sometimes they arrived right in the middle of the destruction. That was how they had found me.

"We were fated to meet," Cate told me. "It is part of the Maker's web. We cannot see the strands as they are being woven, but they form a pattern that connects everything to the center."

"Wise words," I said. "Do they teach all Shamans deep, meaningful sayings when they are apprentices?"

Cate rolled her eyes and tapped my shoulder, the one that the kerak had not injured. I tapped her back. A day after my discovery, I was still in a state of ecstasy. I could joke, laugh, and smile again. Colors seemed brighter. Food tasted better. Even the air seemed sweeter. Just the knowledge I would return to free Raisa had undone a year's worth of sorrow.

"I have no idea. I didn't have an average apprenticeship. I lived in Seria for most of my life." Her face fell, and my smile disappeared along with hers.

"You didn't like it there, did you? I've never been there, but I did grow up near the border." My nose wrinkled at the memory of Byron. "I know that Serians don't trust *Ariada*."

Cate shrugged. "Not all Serians. Some are *Ariada* themselves. My best friend still lives there, and she can speak with animals. In fact, she is the one I was telling you about earlier. It's thanks to her that I was able to find the spell you needed."

"Then I owe her my thanks as well. I've been looking for a way to free Raisa for over a year."

Cate's eyes grew wide, and she stared over my shoulder at the distant outline of the mountains. "Raisa. That's the name of the girl you are trying to help, isn't it? Mogra imprisoned her."

I should not have been surprised Cate already knew so much of my history, but it was still unsettling, especially since I had not spoken Raisa or Mogra's names. Shamans were rare, even among *Ariada*, and the style of magic Cate had been born with was completely unfamiliar to me.

"Yes. Mother—" Her name felt awkward on my tongue. "I mean, Mogra…she trapped Raisa in a cave. I have to find a way to break the enchantment and free her."

Cate drifted back to herself, and her forehead creased with worry. "You might need the services of an Enchanter, then. I'm surprised Mogra was able to bind her at all. From what I know of her, she is a Shaper."

"She's more than just a Shaper. She already knows at least three of the seven arts." I lowered my eyes into my lap. "And while I wouldn't go so far as to call myself a real Enchanter, I know enough to use shape-magic."

One of Cate's hands folded over mine, but I could not bring myself to look up at her. "You walk a dangerous path, Ailynn. The seven types of magic are kept separate for a reason. To seize more power than you were given leads to pride, and pride leads to corruption. Once you have that kind of influence…"

"I know. I saw what Mogra became."

"But do you know what she's done?" Something in Cate's voice forced me to meet her eyes, and the pain I saw there pierced my chest. She drew my hand out of my lap and rested it beneath the hem of her shirt, where the wolf skin belt broke the smooth expanse of her skin. Her flesh was unnaturally warm, and threads of magic curled around my fingers. "She was the one who turned me into a Wyr. I was lucky. The Farseer pack rescued me before she warped my mind along with my body."

I stared at her in horror. Mogra's words came back to me, twisting themselves into my ears. *'I have been making things. Wonderful things. Terrible things.'* The wolf's howl I had heard just outside of her cave that night had not been a coincidence. Neither were the cages lining the walls. I shuddered, trying not to imagine Cate in one of them. My hand jerked away from her stomach as though it had been burned. "I…I had no idea. I am so sorry."

Cate gave me a smile. "There is no reason for you to be sorry. In a strange way, Mogra actually made my life better. I like who I am, and if she hadn't abducted me, I never would have met Larna or joined the Farseer pack."

"That doesn't excuse what she did."

"Of course not. Wyr are not even the worst of her creations."

Dread crept over me. "The kerak," I murmured. "Mogra Shaped them, too."

"Yes, along with the shadowkin. She is building the Queen an army."

My shoulders slumped, and I twisted my hands together in my lap. "I should have put it together before now. I know she's insane, but sometimes I have trouble connecting the horrible person she is now with the person she used to be. She wasn't always like this."

"No, she wasn't, and you can never forget it. There is good and evil in everyone, and only our choices show what we really are. Magic is only as good as its user."

I forced myself to look at Cate again. Perhaps if I made the promise aloud, to someone other than myself, I would be more likely to keep it.

"After I free Raisa, no more Enchanting. I won't become my mother."

Cate gave my knee a brief squeeze and stood up. "No, I'm certain you won't. I don't even need magic to predict that. Come on, let's get back to camp. The sun is starting to set."

Rae D. Magdon

CHAPTER THREE

WE SPENT THE NEXT day helping the villagers to rebuild their town. Larna spent much of her time working in the city itself, leaving Cate to tend to the injured. Since I also possessed a great deal of herbal and medical knowledge, I took it upon myself to ease some of her burden. She was grateful for the help, and even asked me several questions as I worked, seeking to expand her own skills.

At midday, we stopped to take a short break outside. Cate found a patch of grass outside the tents the fire had not destroyed, and I joined her. I had opened up to my rescuer and nurse during the past two days, filling in the pieces of my history she did not already Know. I found myself talking about Raisa frequently. To my relief, Cate accepted my rambling with polite interest and tolerated my impatience.

"When will I be well enough to travel?" I asked her. "I want to see Raisa again as soon as possible."

Setting down her mug of tea, Cate ran her fingers through her hair, attempting to bring some order to her wild red curls. The color of her hair and her bright green eyes made her look like a true child of Amendyr. "Why are you asking me? You know much more about healing than I do." I had not touched my own tea. She nudged it towards me, a not-very-subtle reminder. "When do you think you will be ready to ride a horse?"

"That changes things," I said, accepting the cup and taking a small sip. I had not been fond of tea since Mother had drugged me, but I was too polite to refuse Cate's hospitality. "I was expecting to walk, but if I'm riding, I should be well enough to leave tomorrow." In truth, I was not yet strong enough to leave, but I could not bear to wait another day.

Raisa needed me. I needed her just as badly. "It's been so long since I last saw her. I wonder if she's all right? If she's changed. Part of me is absolutely certain she will welcome me back, but I'm still afraid. I didn't leave under the best circumstances."

Cate took another long drink of her tea and closed her eyes. The steam rising from the cup washed over her face, bringing more color to her freckled cheeks. "You ran away. But perhaps that is for the best. You blame yourself for abandoning her, but I think you needed to leave. You could not be her keeper forever."

I shifted my eyes away from Cate, uncomfortable with the direction of the conversation. "I didn't have a choice. I had to find a way to break the binding spell."

"That wasn't what I meant. I'm going to give you some advice. It has nothing to do with Knowing and everything to do with your own descriptions of your relationship."

I almost told Cate her advice was unwelcome, but I could not bring myself to snap at her. Since she offered the guidance in a calm, friendly spirit, I relented. "All right."

Cate took a breath. "Don't allow Raisa to become swallowed up in you, Ailynn. She was only a baby when you first met her, and you became her whole world. Since you left, she has had to stand on her own for an entire year without you. You were her guardian and friend before you were her lover, and having so much of yourself wrapped up in another person can be frightening."

For some reason, I sensed Cate was not just talking about Raisa and me anymore. "Is that what happened with you and Larna?"

Cate nodded. "To a small extent. We fell in love quickly, and I was still emotionally weak after recovering from painful events in my past. My friend Ellie, who owned the book I gave you, had started to show me how to be my own person with my own wants and needs. Then I went and fell in love before I had a chance to discover who I was." She smiled. "I was consumed by Larna. I was deliriously happy, but a small part of me was still discontent."

"But you worked through your problems?"

"Yes. Our love was more than strong enough, but there were a few times when I had to remind myself I was more than just half of a whole. It was difficult finding a balance at first, and Larna and I had our fair share of fights, but she was supportive and attentive to my needs."

Secretly, I was relieved that Cate and Larna, who seemed like the perfect pair, sometimes fought and struggled. It made me feel more confident. "Maybe being *Tuathe* doesn't guarantee that everything will be perfect."

Cate set her cup aside and leaned back onto the grass, her hair spreading out in an auburn fan behind her head. "Nothing can guarantee happiness, Ailynn, even a soul mate. You must seek it within yourself. But being *Tuathe*, having a love you can depend on and draw strength from, should be a help instead of a hindrance." Cate sounded wise far beyond her years, and I was struck once again by the strange, ageless quality of her knowledge.

I smiled. "So, you're telling me not to stop Raisa from changing as a person, even if it frightens me?"

Cate turned her head to look at me and grinned. "And once again, you have summarized several minutes of complex advice into a single sentence. You make me sound foolish, Ailynn." She sighed, staring up into the sky. White clouds floated across the endless landscape of blue, carried by the breeze. "Oh, that one looks like a hare," she said, pointing up to show me.

"As long as you don't try to eat it," I said, amused by the sudden change of topic. The first time I had seen Cate devour raw meat had been both shocking and unpleasant, to say the least.

"No," she said. "I am happy with my tea for now. You, however, still haven't finished yours. I made it just for you so you would be able to sleep well tonight."

Guilted into action, I took a second, longer sip, trying not to remember the past. For the first time in a long time, I could look toward the future instead.

* * *

Although her manner and words were simpler, Larna also imparted some knowledge to me on the night before I left camp. We were cleaning up after a large dinner, gathering bowls and simple traveling cutlery to be washed. "Cate tells me that you are leaving us tomorrow," she said, breaking the silence between us as we worked. "Are you sure you be well enough to travel?"

I adjusted the weight of the dishes in my hand, turning to face her. Although I had formed a quick friendship with Cate during the past several days of my recovery, Larna and I had not able to spend as much time together. She was always busy organizing something or helping someone, tending to the responsibilities of leadership.

"I need to go back," I said, allowing her to relieve me of my stack of dishes.

Together, we began rinsing out the bowls, using damp rags to wipe them clean. The simple chore, almost automatic, reminded me of home. Although I missed Raisa terribly, I also missed Mother. That surprised me.

"Ailynn? Are you all right?"

I looked up, staring into concerned brown eyes. I found it touching that someone who did not know me very well was asking after my happiness. Living alone in the forest, I had not been given many opportunities to make friends. "I'm worried. How did you know?"

Larna shrugged. "You have been after washing the same bowl three times." Her accent was much more pronounced than Cate's. I guessed she had grown up somewhere along the coast or closer to the center of Amendyr, away from the border.

"I don't know what is troubling me," I lied, not really wanting to discuss it. Truthfully, I thought about Raisa and how I had left her. Cate's conversation from earlier in the day played in my head. Although I wanted to return to my *Tuathe*, I did not know what kind of welcome I would receive. What if Raisa felt cheated of her final moments with me? What if she was upset I had been gone so long? Worse still, what if I had been wrong, and Mogra had found a reason to hurt her? "I want to go back. I'm just afraid."

Larna took the bowl from my hand and passed me a new one. "Afraid? Of what?"

"It's been a year since I left Raisa. I'm afraid something's happened to her." Larna gave me a doubtful look, and I bit down on my lower lip. "And I'm even more afraid that she won't take me back. I abandoned her, even though I did it to try and save her."

"You feel guilty." Again, Larna's voice made me look up. I set my bowl and rag aside. "Stop. Love forgives. So will she." The rest of her words remained unspoken, but I still understood. I could only hope she was right.

* * *

"You look tired." Cate brushed back a lock of my hair and tucked it behind my ear. "Those are dark circles under your eyes. Are you sure you will be all right on a horse?"

"More than all right," I assured her. I had been unable to sleep during the night, too preoccupied with what the morning would bring. Of course, the passionate sounds drifting over from Cate and Larna's tent beside mine had not helped my situation, but I was too embarrassed to mention it. I looked away from her to hide my blush, staring out over the plains instead. The sun's pink edge was just visible on the horizon.

Cate shook her head, but she handed over the reins of a middle-aged quarter horse, patting him affectionately on his rump. The horse twitched, uncomfortable with Cate's touch, and she sighed. "Horses have not liked me since the change. I wish that Ellie were here. She might be able to convince them I only want to ride them, not eat them."

"He still lets you handle him. That counts for something."

"They are even more frightened of us when we change. They start whickering all through the camp. Sometimes it takes an entire candlemark to calm them down." I could not blame the horses, I thought to myself. I had only seen Cate's half-shape form once, and I still remembered the terror it had stirred in me. Careful to move slowly so she did not startle the horse, Cate began checking my saddlebags and traveling packs. "Do you have everything?"

I rolled my eyes. "Yes. This is the third time you have asked."

"You have the book I gave you?"

"Yes."

Cate frowned as the horse stomped one hoof. "Well, I went through a lot of trouble to get it for you, and I don't want you to leave it here." A curious look crossed her face, and for a moment, her hazy eyes seemed to see far beyond me. "But try not to worry. I'm sure Ellie will forgive you if you lose it."

I shook my head. "Not likely. That book was the answer to my prayers. I seriously doubt I'll be careless enough to lose it." Placing my foot in the stirrups, I swung my leg over the large creature's back, shifting into a comfortable position in the saddle. Riding was another skill I had gained during my year away from home. I still remembered the first time I had dismounted a horse and discovered the most difficult part was walking on sore legs afterwards.

"Larna and I will be traveling to the west, past Catyr Bane, on a diplomatic mission. Jett Bahari wants us to ask the Liarre for their help. If you need to find me, that is where I will be." The curious expression of secret, guarded knowledge remained on her face, and I wondered if Cate Knew something I did not.

"Have you seen the Liarre before?" The half-human, half-animal hybrids had always fascinated me from a historical standpoint as well as a magical one.

"No, but we have been in communication with them for a while. We think that they will receive Wyr diplomats better than human ones."

"Aren't you a little young to be a diplomat?"

Cate grinned. "Were you picturing an old man with a grey beard?" I shrugged. "One more thing. After you finish playing the knight-errant and rescue the maiden, you might consider coming back to join us. We have need of skilled *Ariada* in the rebellion, and you would be more than welcome in my sickroom. You know even more than I do about herbs."

I sighed. Although we had only known each other a short time, Cate and Larna already seemed like friends to me, and I did not have many. I also liked the idea of helping to undo some of the damage caused by Mogra. But Raisa had to be my priority. I would go wherever she wanted to me to go. "I am flattered, but I cannot leave Raisa again."

"Bring her with you. There are several women and children with us now. Honestly, there is no safer place for you to be. With the Queen's creatures burning cities and destroying villages, you stand a better chance with an army to protect you."

"I will ask her," I promised. "Cate, thank you. Thank you for giving me back my soul."

Cate accepted the words with a small smile. "You are most welcome, Ailynn Gothel. Let the Maker watch over you. I am sure we will meet again."

I prodded the horse's sides with my heels and urged him into a brisk walk, turning around to give my friend a last wave goodbye. Although I had no trace of the Sight, I suspected we would see each other again.

CHAPTER FOUR

MY JOURNEY HOME WAS surprisingly short, and thinking of Raisa made it seem even shorter. With a clear destination, I could ride in a straight line instead of traveling in zigzags from village to village. The horse Cate had given me was not very quick, but what he lacked in speed, he made up for in strength and endurance. I struggled far more than he did after a long day of riding, but the extra hours he was able to travel added up quickly. Within six days I found myself nearing the edge of the forest.

The sights, sounds, and smells past the tree line welcomed me in an embrace after a year away. Everything else in my life had changed, but at least this was still the same. Suppressing feelings of nostalgia, I dismounted and led my horse carefully through the trees. He shuffled back and forth, clearly uncomfortable in such close quarters, and resisted when I tried to guide him with a tug on his reins. "Sorry, boy," I murmured. "I promise we won't be staying long."

Traveling on foot was much slower going, and it took me most of the daylight hours to penetrate the forest's outer edge. The deeper into the forest we went, the more familiar it became. Before I knew it, I was on the path that led to Raisa's cave. As I approached its mouth, my doubts grew stronger. After waiting so long for this moment, it almost seemed impossible that I was finally here, finally home. It looked no different than when I had departed on that grey morning over a year ago.

My hands shook as I tied the horse's reins to the branch of a tree and checked the ground. There was the edge of Raisa's braid, the same as always. I breathed a sigh of relief. Part of me had been afraid she wouldn't be here waiting for me. I gathered my courage, summoned my fire, and headed down into the darkness.

I followed the golden thread of Raisa's hair through the twisting pathways, and soon, I could see the edge of the cavern. I smiled, lifting my voice in excitement. "Raisa?" There was no answer. "Raisa, are you there?" I waited for several heartbeats, but there was only silence and stillness. I glanced down and noticed that the braid ended just outside the door. Rapunzel had recently cut her hair, or… perhaps Mogra had taken her away and left her hair behind. I gritted my teeth, wrestling the fear into submission. I would not start panicking until I saw for myself. Unable to wait any longer, I opened the door. Raisa was there, but she was not alone.

A nightmare. It had to be a nightmare. Some twisted construct of my imagination. A man lay on top of her. The pale skin of his naked back burned into my eyes. His hips pumped in a jagged rhythm, blonde hair tossing as he moved. And Raisa was beneath him. I couldn't make out her face, but I could still see her. At first, I feared he was hurting her, but before I could force my legs to move, I saw her hands trail along his shoulders.

Hot tears streamed down my cheeks. My hands clenched tighter and tighter, wishing they were around his throat. Then he said her name. The name that had haunted me for the entire year we had spent apart. The name that should have been kept for my lips alone. I could not watch anymore. The broken pieces of my heart sank to the bottom of my chest. I must have made a sound, must have given some sort of voice to my grief and betrayal, because Raisa jerked below him. Our eyes met, and her mouth opened in shock. Color bled into her pale cheeks. She screamed, and the man stopped moving to look as well.

I wanted to leave, to run as far and as fast as the winds took me, but I found myself stepping forward instead. Twenty-two years. Twenty-two years I had waited for this moment, this woman. He had stolen it. I hated him. For the first and only time in my life, I wondered if my mother had been right to lock Raisa away from the world. She should have been mine. She should have been kept safe for me, for me only.

I did not realize Raisa was near me until I felt her hand on my cheek. Although she mouthed my name, I could not hear her through the roar in my ears. I shuddered and wrenched myself away. She had betrayed me. I did not want her tenderness.

The man stood perfectly still beside her, stupid as stone, not even bothering to cover his nakedness. The sight of him sickened me. Mother would have killed him. Mother would have cut off his fingers for stealing what did not belong to him. It was a punishment fit for a thief, but I could always adapt it and cut off something else instead. I did not need to speak my Word of Power to feed the blaze around my hands. It flared up on its own, feeding from my anger, eating away at my skin as my heart crumbled to ashes.

My fire must have terrified him, or else he read my murderous intentions in my eyes. He shoved me aside and ran, naked as a dog, out of the cavern and into the cave beyond. I could not bring myself to follow him, but I hoped he would lose himself in the twisting tunnels and never see the light of day again. I did not turn away or stifle the flames dancing between my fingers until he was well out of sight.

That left me alone with her. My Raisa. But no longer mine, not anymore. She was speaking, but my ears filled with the loud, wordless roar of anger. I watched her lips move, mesmerized and furious. Tears of fire burned in my eyes, searing my cheeks and chin, blazing down my neck. Finally, one of her words broke through. "Ailynn…"

"Don't." My voice cracked. I swallowed against the painful lump in my throat. I did not want to hear her say my name.

"Ailynn, please listen."

I gripped the back of her neck, dragging her forward and silencing her with my lips. The kiss was hard, bruising, possessive. She melted under my touch, quivering with what could have been pain or fear or love. I had no idea anymore. "I hate you," I whispered, biting into the curve of her lower lip with my teeth.

Raisa flinched against my chest, but did not pull away. "As long as you feel something."

She was right. I felt too much. Her face. Those eyes. I thought I saw love written there, but after what I had witnessed, how could that be? My mind shut down, and I surrendered to my body instead. Despite everything, I still wanted her. Here she was, the woman I thought I had loved, naked and trembling in my arms after more than a year apart. The warmth and sweetness of her unsteady breaths made me want to kiss her again. I could not live with the knowledge that some disgusting stranger had been the last one to touch her. My chest still ached with the pain of what I had lost—what we had lost—but I did not care.

I shoved her backwards, sending her sprawling onto the bed. She did not protest. Instead, she reached out for me, trying to catch my wrist and pull me with her. I stayed back and tore at my clothes, searing through the fabric when it did not loosen fast enough. Raisa did not flinch. She remained perfectly still, waiting for a kiss, or perhaps even a blow. I wanted her still, and I hated myself for it. I needed to take back the piece of me she had stolen.

I grabbed for her as soon as I climbed onto the bed. I dug in with my nails, tearing her skin as I raked over her thighs. I took her throat in my teeth and nipped the white, unblemished skin, making her mewl like a kitten. I would leave my mark on her, the woman who should have been mine. As my lips claimed her throat, my fingers found the rest, sliding between her legs. I stopped short as soon as I felt her wetness, remembering every touch I had seen him give her. Was it for him, or for me?

I hated the way Raisa's hips pushed into my touch, the way her warmth spilled over my hand. My stomach lurched, but the rest of my body shook with want. I hated that I still desired her so much, but I could not continue touching her in anger. Something in my heart blocked me from satisfying that fearsome urge. Though I had handled her roughly, I could not bear to cause her any more pain, or think of her as an object to be claimed. I did not own her, and I would not force her.

"I can't," I stammered, moving to pull away.

"No, don't." Raisa's hand cupped over mine, holding it in place. Before I could process what was happening, two of my fingers pushed inside of her. Burning silk clutched down around me, and I could not bear to try and pull back again. "I love you. I'm yours."

My heart stopped. So did my breath. The words were even more overwhelming than being inside of her at last. My anger burnt out. It seared an empty hollow in my chest that cried out to be filled. "Tell me again," I whispered. Despite everything, I wanted to hear her say it.

"I love you, Ailynn. I'm yours."

I felt the pain of my heart breaking all over again. Or was it mending? I did not care. Shockwaves rippled through my entire body, radiating from the aching pool between my legs to the very tips of my fingers and toes. I wrapped my other hand in her hair, feeling the silken strands. She was still the same person I had longed for, and at least for now, she was mine once more. "Again. Please. I need to hear."

"Let me show you instead." Her hand tightened over mine to keep my fingers buried inside of her. My heartbeat jerked in the base of my throat as smooth, warm muscle pulsed around me. "I'm yours, Ailynn. I always have been."

Having her ask for my touch and offer herself to me called back the rush of possessiveness I had felt before. I floated in the sensation, soaking in the pleasure of being with this woman. I would make her forget, erase that man and everyone else from her memory and sear myself into her until she could not part herself from me. I climbed over her, settling myself tightly between her thighs. One of her legs wrapped around my waist, and I began to move inside of her, gently this time. I kissed her breath away, making sure her eyes were open so she could see exactly who was touching her.

I had no idea what I was doing at first. Other than touching myself, I had no frame of reference. But as I listened to the sounds she made, I began to learn her body. The harder I pressed, the more urgently she rocked back against my hand. I tried thrusting at first, but quickly discovered that curling worked better. She was so slick, so tight around me, and jealousy began to eat at my heart once again. He might have known Raisa's body first, but I would learn to please her better.

I began searching higher, and her hips shot up from the mattress when I finally found what I was looking for. "Ailynn!" The sound of my name falling from her lips made my pelvis jerk against hers. The need growing inside of me was nearly impossible to ignore, but I forced it down. I drank in her responses instead—the sharp break in her voice as she sobbed my name, the bruising grip of her fingers along my shoulders, and the swollen point that twitched against the pad of my thumb. All proof she wanted me.

I forced myself to tease her, to trace around the throbbing bundle of nerves without stroking its tip. Raisa writhed beneath me and tightened her knee around my waist. Her other thigh slid between my legs, and my breath caught. A powerful ripple started deep within me, and I froze, too overwhelmed to keep touching her. Raisa did not seem to care. She pushed her hips forward one last time, catching herself against my thumb and taking the rest of my fingers as deep as she could.

Her body went rigid as her release came crashing down. She clung to me as though I was her only tie to the world. Her nails scoured my shoulders, but I barely noticed the pain. All I knew was sharp fluttering around my fingers and surge of wetness flooding into my hand. Something within me shattered, and I pushed hard against her knee, desperate for purchase. All of the heat inside me overflowed, and I screamed, taking her lips in another fierce kiss.

At last, the sharp contractions inside of me began fading to aftershocks. I was embarrassed by the dripping mess I had made on A lump rose in my throat Raisa's thigh, as well as the warmth that had spilled past my wrist, but I hardly had time to acknowledge them.

Raisa's hips stopped their rolling motion, and she broke our kiss, panting heavily against the curve of my neck. Our hearts beat together. She looked up at me with bright, shining eyes, and her lips curved in a wide smile. It was a truthful face, overflowing with love and joy. "I love you, Ailynn. Now and always."

I buried my face in her hair and cried, allowing her to cradle me in her warm arms and stroke my back. There would be time for explanations later. For now, all I wanted was to be with Raisa again. I would not be foolish enough to lose her a second time.

CHAPTER FIVE

I DID NOT KNOW how long we stayed there together, just breathing, just being. I was overjoyed to see Raisa again, solid and real in my arms. But that man haunted me. The fresh memory burrowed into my mind, eating away at me and leaving me hollow. Some of my old anger resurfaced. I untangled myself from Raisa's arms, retreating to the other side of the bed. I could not bear to be so close.

"Why?" I asked at last. The lonely word hung between us.

Raisa's eyes darted away from mine, but not before I saw the guilt there. "I had to find a way out." She reached out, pushing back a lock of hair that clung to my cheek and tucking it behind my ear. The tender gesture almost made me break into a fresh round of tears. "I never meant to hurt you, but I thought if Byron—"

Byron. The image of a small blonde boy with a turned-up nose came flooding back to me. Him? How had he even found her after all these years? Why had Raisa chosen him over me? "What about him made you want—? Why couldn't I—?" As hard as I tried, I could not form sentences. The questions formed a painful tangle in my mind, and I could not pick out the knots.

"I thought you were dead."

The quiet statement stole the breath from my chest. Raisa had thought I was dead? "What on earth made you think that?" I asked, unsure whether to be surprised or angry. Even if I had died, it hurt to know Raisa had let go of my memory so quickly. Had I meant anything at all to her? I still loved her, as much as I wanted to deny it, but had returning been a mistake? Maybe I should have left her for Byron. She might have been better off that way.

"Mother Gothel told me. Ailynn, she's gotten worse."

I squeezed my eyes shut to keep from crying. I did not want to know what was happening with my mother. She had lost my respect and trust long ago, and I still felt guilty for leaving Raisa, trapped and alone, under her power.

"She told me you were dead, that you were never coming back. I couldn't stay in this cave forever. When Byron found this place, I hoped I could convince him to buy her off and take me away. You know how she is about her treasures."

A lump rose in my throat, but I swallowed it down, and the sharp edge of my pain faded to a dull ache. "So, what I saw was—"

"Me trying to negotiate for my freedom. I don't love Byron. I never loved him. I am not proud of what we did. It was not indescribably terrible, but I took no pleasure in it. During the moments when I couldn't bear it anymore, I tried to imagine you. You are the only one I have ever loved, Ailynn."

I had no idea whether Raisa's confession made things better or worse. I was relieved that she still loved me, but disgust crashed over me as well at the means she had used to try and secure her freedom. But could I blame her? If I was hidden away in a cave with almost no hope of escape, and believed my love and only possible savior was dead, I could not say what I would have done. The logical part of me understood Raisa had seen a chance for survival and taken it, but my heart did not understand at all.

"I don't know what you want me to say," I mumbled.

Raisa cupped my cheeks in her hands and kissed me. It was a complete contrast to the way I had kissed her before. There was no hunger or possessiveness, only a light, soft brushing of lips. "Don't say anything," she whispered. "Don't think about the future. Just tell me that now, while we are alone together and there is no one else to come between us, tell me that you love me."

"I love you," I told her. "I just don't know if love is enough." I caught the flash of hurt in her eyes, and it almost made me want to take back my words. But I owed her the truth, if nothing else.

"Do you love me enough to try?" she asked.

That was a question I could answer. No matter what she had done, I could not simply leave her. I owed it to both of us to see if I could forgive her. Cautiously, I reached out to touch her. I followed the curve of her side with my hand, amazed at the warmth of her body and the softness of her skin. Even though her appearance had not changed much during my absence, something seemed different about her. Cate was right. While I was gone, Raisa had become a woman. "I'll try," I whispered. "But I feel like I've lost so much of you while I was away. You've changed."

Raisa's hand covered mine, holding it against her bare hip. "Oh, Ailynn, please don't be afraid. You haven't lost me. I might have changed, but my feelings haven't."

"What do you dream of? What do you want for your future?"

"I want to see places. I have always wanted to visit Kalmarin. I want to learn every story and song in the world, and I want to draw pictures to go along with them."

I raised my eyebrows in surprise. "You want to draw?" I repeated, making sure I had heard correctly.

"Yes. When I ran out of books, I had to pick up a new hobby." She shifted beside me, swinging her legs over the side of the bed and standing up. I could not help admiring her retreating form as she walked over to the writing desk where I had left my goodbye note. Her figure was rounder, fuller, with a slight curve to her belly I found strangely attractive.

I tore my eyes away from her and noticed that the moonflowers I had given her were still alive. Their buds were closed, but they seemed to be healthy. "You kept them?" I asked, standing up from the bed and following her over to the desk.

Raisa turned and gave me a sad smile. "Of course I did. I've kept several things to remind me of you." She pulled something out of a drawer and turned around to face me. "Here, look," she said, holding out several loosely bound sheets of paper.

I took them from her and examined the first page, surprised to see my own face staring back at me. It was not exactly as I knew myself—my lips were fuller, my eyes larger, my hair as luxurious as my mother's used to be at the height of her glory—but the detail with which she had captured my features amazed me. Did she truly see me this way? The woman in this sketch was breathtaking.

Carefully, I turned to the next page. Another drawing of me, showing my entire body this time, a forest behind my figure. My heart skipped. I flipped through the rest of the pages, unable to stop myself. There were a few other drawings—the petals of a moonflower, a sunset, and some landscapes. Aside from them, the entire collection featured me.

"These are amazing," I breathed in wonder. "I can't believe you drew them."

Raisa gripped her elbow with her hand and glanced down, embarrassed by the praise. "I didn't want to forget your face. I was so terrified of that. I had nightmares about it." A blush crawled across her cheeks, and she cleared her throat, staring over at the wall. "There are more drawings on the bottom of the stack."

Curious, I turned to the last few drawings. This time, my mouth fell open. These pictures were also of me, but they were clearly not from any memories of our shared past. Me unclothed, posed on my side and smiling. Me sleeping, sheets tangled around my ankles, revealing everything. Me straddling Raisa, holding her wrists over her head with one hand as the other worked between her legs. It was the first time Raisa had appeared in her own drawings. She was in the next one, too, with her head buried between my thighs. I looked at image after image of us laughing, touching, making love.

"Oh my." Heat crept over my cheeks, embarrassed by my own surprised exclamation and acutely aware of the fact that both of us were still naked. That embarrassment quickly transformed into something else. I was sitting in bed, naked, with the woman I loved only a few feet away from me, and I was looking at drawings? Beautiful drawings, but nevertheless...*Oh my, indeed.*

I snuck a glance at Raisa, and she stared at me with a longing expression on her face that I could not say no to her. The painful discussions and soul-searching could wait. It would take time to see if we could repair the damage done, but for now, there was only us. I opened my arms, welcoming her as she slid into them. Her fingers wove through my hair, and she leaned in close. "I love you," she murmured against my lips. I did not return the words, because I did not want her to misinterpret them, but a tiny part of my broken heart began to heal.

Our mouths collided in an urgent kiss, one that quickly spiraled beyond our control. As our lips played together in an endless game of tease and taste, my palms explored the smooth landscape of her back. I memorized every inch of skin I could reach, folding my hands around her hips. I pulled her on top of me until she was straddling my waist, and I gasped as warmth pressed against my belly. It was the same velvety heat from before, but this time, it was all because of me.

Raisa stared down at me with hazy, lust-filled eyes, but her shuddering breaths revealed she felt as nervous and unsteady as I did. Wordlessly seeking permission, she reached down to trace the curve of my breasts. Her curious, hesitant touch was too frightening, too powerful. I pushed her away. She looked disappointed until I cupped a hand between our bodies, finding her with my fingers. I smiled as the proof of her desire coated my hand, filling me with pride.

"Please," I whispered. "We don't have to stop. I want to touch you again."

Raisa leaned back, locking her arms to stay upright and catch her balance. "You can touch me however you like."

Instead of taking the invitation right away, I stole a glance between her legs. Although I had touched Raisa before, I had not really taken the opportunity to look at her. During the last several months before my departure, I had spent many feverish nights imagining what she would look like completely naked, but my fantasies paled in comparison with reality. Her outer lips were full and swollen, pouting open to reveal the smooth, shimmering pink of her inner folds. I could not see her entrance, but the hard red point of her clit was obvious, peeking out from beneath its thin hood.

"You're beautiful," I murmured, spreading her further apart with my hand. That, at least, I could say.

I wanted to see all of her, to know all of her. Two of my fingers slipped forward, quickly swallowed by heated silk. She shifted further back, spreading her legs even wider, and I let out a whimper as I watched my fingers disappear inside of her. She hissed at the stretch, but the new fullness coaxed out another pulse of heat from deep within her. She slid one of her hands down along her stomach, and my eyes widened in surprise when she began teasing the swollen bud of her clit. Her gaze met mine for a moment, waiting for my response, and I nodded. She looked beautiful.

She began rocking urgently against my hand, setting a much faster rhythm than I expected. This was an exorcism. Just as I had tried to claim Raisa roughly before, wanting to drive out the memories of Byron's touch with every thrust inside of her, she was reclaiming herself with each tilt of her hips. She stared down into my eyes, and pleasure and love eclipsed the painful memory.

Watching Raisa slide onto my fingers made my heart swell. Her chin tilted back, and I could see the curve of her pale throat and the purple shadow that pooled in the dip of her collarbone. She arched her back, pushing her breasts forward, and I could not resist leaning up and taking a pink nipple between my lips. Her inner muscles squeezed even tighter as my teeth grazed the sensitive bud. I pushed up to meet her thrusts, driving my fingers into the swollen spot along her front wall.

At last, Raisa stiffened above me. Her slick inner muscles pulsed around me, I pushed as deep inside of her as I could. A tide of warmth spilled into my palm, running over my hand and down onto my stomach. Her fingers stiffened against her clit, and I brushed them aside, rubbing the swollen pearl myself. This time, her whimper became a scream. Her body seized and shivered. She was the most beautiful thing I had ever seen.

Once I had coaxed out everything she had to give, Raisa collapsed on top of me, trying to catch her breath. I eased her down from her high, stroking her hair and murmuring sweet words against the pink shell of her ear. As she came back to the world, her eyes focused on me. I shivered as they roamed over my breasts, my stomach, my legs. I observed her in return, pleased to notice that she looked disheveled and very well loved.

"You needed that," I said, letting my hand rest over the swell of her backside as she curled up against me. The weight in my chest already seemed a little lighter.

Raisa smiled, tracing patterns against my thighs with her fingertips. The barely-there touch made my legs tense. "I did. But now I want to please you." Her hand crept higher, but I caught her wrist. The fullness between my legs ached with each breath I took, and my muscles shivered in anticipation, but I could not let go of my fear. "Oh, Ailynn," she murmured against my neck, "Please let me touch you."

"I can't," I stuttered, ashamed of myself. The look of disappointment on Raisa's face was a knife in my heart. "I'm still hurting. Give me some time." Although she did not pull away from me, Raisa turned her head so that it was buried in a pillow, hiding her eyes. Her hand found safer territory, wrapping around my waist instead. I tried to retrace my steps and erase the damage, but it was already too late. "I'm sorry."

"No, I'm sorry," Raisa sighed. "I hoped—"

"That everything would fix itself. I hoped that would happen, too." I paused, wondering whether to give voice to thoughts I knew were true, but had not yet accepted in my heart. "I know that you only did what you thought you needed to. But—"

"But?"

"But it still hurts."

Raisa raised her head from the pillow and looked at me. "I will do everything I can to ease your doubts, Ailynn, no matter how long it takes."

CHAPTER SIX

I AWOKE, STARTLED AND bathed in a cold sweat. For a moment I did not remember where I was, but as something warm moved against my side, the memories came back. Raisa slept peacefully beside me. The moonflower's blossoms had closed, and sun streamed in through the enchanted ceiling. We had spent the entire night wrapped in each other's arms.

I leaned over to stroke her hair, brushing my lips across her forehead. She did not move. I shifted across the mattress as carefully as possible, but despite my efforts, she felt me stir. "Go back to sleep, dear heart," she mumbled into the pillow, trying to loop an arm around my waist and pull me back against her side.

"But it's already morning," I whispered. "You can stay in bed. I need to get something." I stretched my arms up to the ceiling, popping my spine with a loud crack, and stifled a shiver as the soles of my bare feet touched the stone floor.

Raisa opened one eye to watch me. "What is so important that you need to leave me again?" Her voice remained calm, but I caught the hint of fear behind her eyes. She was still afraid I would abandon her. She had not even asked about my search for the binding spell. Perhaps she was afraid I would need to leave again and continue my search.

"Go back to bed," I insisted, bending over to pick up my discarded clothes. The waistband of my leggings had been stretched out of shape and one sleeve of my shirt was singed.

Raisa shifted on the bed, letting the sheets fall away from her body. Her lips twitched into a seductive smile. "But I'm enjoying the view. I need all the references I can get for my drawings, you know."

I snorted, secretly pleased. "I'm only going outside to check on the horse. I'll be back in a few minutes." I did not want to tell Raisa about the book yet. Although I had skimmed the relevant section several times, I still needed to examine the specific spell linking Raisa to the cave. I understood what needed to be done, but putting magical theory into practice, especially one concerning a discipline not my own, would be far from simple.

Raisa did not question me further. Perhaps she sensed my reluctance to talk about it. I was confident I could release her from her prison, but I did not want to raise her hopes only to disappoint her if I failed. Both of us had already been through enough already. As I looked for my shoes, Raisa's breathing evened out, and she drifted back into a light sleep. I could not help glancing over my shoulder. *Soon. Soon, I will be able to take you away from this place.*

I followed her severed braid back through the tunnels. The journey seemed to take longer this time, and the further I went from Raisa, the more my heart sank. I already missed her. Memories of the night before crept into my mind, and my stomach lurched as I pictured Byron's face. I could still see him on top of her, where I should have been, and the terror that had overtaken his face upon seeing me gave me little comfort. But then I remembered the way Raisa had whispered my name. How she had knelt over me, gazing down with such love it nearly stopped my heart. My anger and love were all twisted together, and I could not part them.

I did not know what I would do once Raisa and I left the cave. Part of me wanted to run again, as far away as possible, but just the thought of parting from her made my chest ache. No matter what, I was still determined to free her. Breaking Mogra's spell had been my only goal for the past year. I would not abandon it now.

At last, I reached the entrance to the cave. My faithful horse waited for me beside the tree, and a stab of guilt traveled through me for leaving him tied up all night. "Sorry, boy." I stroked his nose and allowing him to lip at my fingers. After I had fed and watered him with my traveling supplies, I removed the saddlebags and gave him a friendly slap on the rump. He cast me a lazy, mournful look before plodding off through the trees, heading for the Forest's edge. Hopefully, his journey back to Cate and the rebellion would be a swift one.

Once he had wandered out of sight, I searched the saddlebags for the thick book Cate had given me. Feeling the texture of its binding as I pulled it out strengthened my resolve. I took a moment to trace the flaking gold lettering that named the book's title, *Elementary Majicks*. I was familiar with it. Mogra's library contained a copy, but the pertinent pages had been torn out and burned. As I flipped open the book to page one ninety-three.

'Linking spells, or binding spells, are used to create a magical 'chain' between two objects, forming a strong bond between them. There are several variations of this spell, which may be used to transfer the properties of one object to another, or may act as a physical tie to make two objects inseparable.

A binding spell may also be used to make an object immovable, a famous historical example being the Sword of the Templars, which cannot be removed from its monastery home in the Northern Sweep. No single Ariada has been able to break that binding spell, because it was made using the combined skill of several monks.

To create a binding spell, the magic-worker must take part of the first object they wish to bind, and combine it with part of the second object. In the aforementioned example, a jewel was taken from the hilt of the Sword of the Templars and submerged in melted glass from the monastery's famous stained-glass windows. Pieces of glass were taken from windows in all parts of the monastery...'

I frowned and stopped reading, scanning the page for more relevant information.

'...must use shape-magic, the art of 'seeing' magical auras with the senses, to tie a knot of magical energy around both small pieces of the objects to be bound, and place these objects in a safe location so that the knot may not be untied. The location must be close to the bound objects...'

My frown relaxed into a smile. It seemed undoing a binding spell was not as complex as making one. If I understood the text correctly, Mogra had taken something from Raisa and combined it with something from the cave. Then, she had woven knots of magic around them like a tangle of string. I only needed to untie the knot.

I felt strangely confident. Although *Elementary Majicks* had said the spell binding the Sword of the Templars to its monastery had not been broken, I doubted Mogra had enlisted the aid of other *Ariada* to create Raisa's binding spell. She was a loner, and did not like associating with other magic-doers unless it was absolutely necessary. If she had used shape-magic to cast the binding spell herself, surely I had the skill to undo it alone.

I closed my eyes and opened the rest of my senses, paying

attention to the vibrating hum of magic surrounding the entrance to the cave. It was like soft music, a sound that could not be distinguished from other noises until I made a conscious decision to focus on its unique timbre. As I came nearer, the buzzing sounds of magic grew louder, vibrating through my skin and warming my bones.

I tossed the heavy book on top of my traveling sack and stretched out my hands. I tried to feel for the strands of magic swirling around the stone, groping blindly through the air. Invisible threads thrummed between my fingers. I followed where they led. Whatever the source, it had to be near the entrance to the cave, where most of it had collected. It was like a childhood game, following the voice of a hiding playmate with closed eyes, listening carefully to choose the right direction. After I had paced inside and outside the cave's entrance three times, I decided that the magic felt strongest just outside the entrance.

I ran my hands along the smooth stones, pushing aside dripping moss to feel the rock beneath. It was surprisingly warm, even against my scarred hands. I bent my knees, following the side of the wall down with my fingers. The texture changed, becoming rougher and pockmarked, as though tiny sparks had eaten away at the rock. I buried my hands in the soft earth and dug, pulling up clods of grass and using the cracked earth to work my fingers deeper into the soil.

Soon, my pants and sleeves were dirty. I had made a shallow, sloping trough of a hole, but my lack of progress frustrated me. Unwilling to give up, I brushed myself off and ran back to my supplies. They remained where I had left them, undisturbed beneath a tree. I rummaged through the saddlebags, searching for the small shovel I used to dig fire pits when I slept in the open.

I found the shovel and hurried back to the humming section of the cave. As I drew closer, I knew I had chosen the right place. The pulses of magic grew stronger, vibrating in the air around me like a deep, calling voice. Soon I had dug an even hole almost three feet deep. Finally, the edge of the shovel collided with something solid. I returned to using my hands, tossing aside earth and brushing the soil away from a flat wooden surface.

As I exposed more of the wood, the magic in the air grew thick enough to fill my lungs, almost burning as it passed over my face. At last, I managed to reveal the smooth edges of a little square box. I tugged until the box came loose, pulling it out of the hole and setting it in my lap. Its wooden sides felt hot to the touch. A few sharp taps of the shovel's blade broke the old lock securing it. Triumphantly, I pulled open the box.

Inside, perched on top of a soft purple cloth, was a lock of golden hair wrapped around a piece of gray stone. I untied the hair, as fresh and healthy as the locks on Raisa's head. The shade matched hers. I would recognize color anywhere. It came loose from the stone, but the steady, insistent hum of magic pouring out of the box did not cease. Closing my eyes again, I reached out with my smudged and dirty hands, trying to feel the threads of magic binding the hair and the stone together. It felt like a tangle of yarn after Sing had made knots and loops playing with it.

I carefully untangled the mess of twists. After a minute, my fingers began to grow sore, but I ignored the stiffness in my joints, wishing I had some invisible scissors. At last, the final loop came undone, and the humming vanished. My head ached from the sudden lack of comforting magical energy. Exhaustion ran through me, but as I threw the stone off into the distance and clambered back to my feet, my strength returned. At last, after years of searching, I had found a way to free my beloved.

I threw off my weariness and kicked the box and the lock of hair aside, forgetting them completely. "Raisa?" I shouted as I hurried back down the sloping tunnel toward the cavern. I fell into a run, only summoning enough light to follow the glimmer of her braid. "Raisa, I've done it!" But as I ran, there was no answer to my call, and her smiling face did not greet me when I finally stood, panting, in front of her door. My wide grin made my cheeks ache, but I did not care. Everything was going to be all right now. None of the bad things mattered anymore. Raisa was free and I was going to take her away from her prison forever.

"Raisa?" I called again, pushing open the door leading to her cavern. There was no answer, but what I saw almost made me stumble backwards and fall down.

She was not alone. Mogra waited for me inside of the cavern room, her hand wrapped around Raisa's throat.

CHAPTER SEVEN

"AILYNN," MOGRA PURRED. "I am not surprised to see you here."

She had forced her lips into a warped smile, but her dark eyes remained cold and unfeeling. The texture of her face wavered between young and old, familiar and unfamiliar. Raisa trembled in her arms, pleading with me to do something, anything. "You would fetch your dearest, but the beautiful bird is no longer singing in the nest."

My hands clenched so tightly I shook with rage. Heat balled in my tight fists, but I did not dare to attack Mogra while she had Raisa trapped. "Let her go," I demanded, praying she still had some shred of her sanity left. "Let both of us leave, and you will never have to deal with me again."

Mogra laughed, a deep, throaty sound that made my stomach flip. The deep grooves in her skin melted away, and she was beautiful again, like a poisonous frog with its lurid colors. In fact, now that I looked more closely, her form had changed from what I remembered. It was a little like a caricature painting from memory, with the details exaggerated.

"Oh, no, I don't think so. The cat has caught your bird and will scratch out your eyes as well. Raisa is lost to you. You will never see her again." If I had any hope left that my mother would regain her sanity and her honor, the last of it was snuffed out like a dying candle. But that did not matter. Only Raisa mattered now.

I raised my fists. Flames jutted out from my bunched knuckles, swimming down my arms in flickering waves of blue and burning away the sleeves of my shirt. I felt no pain, only a cold, stinging fury. I was not a Witch's daughter for nothing. If Mogra tried to hurt Raisa, I would do everything in my power to stop her. "If you don't release her now, I'll make you."

Mogra looked surprised, but not at all afraid. "You dare to use your fire against me a second time? You foolish girl. I am more powerful than you will ever be."

I did not waste my breath on words. Instead, I charged forward. Fire billowed out from my palms as I pushed all of the energy I could summon toward her face. Mogra did not try and stop me. She simply hauled Raisa's body in front of hers, using her as a shield. Raisa screamed, and my eyes widened in terror. I tugged at the humming strands of magic around me, struggling to pull the tongues of flame back up along my arms. My fire obeyed, but it left my skin aching with unbearable heat.

Mogra tightened her grip on Raisa's neck. "Enough of this game." She lifted her hand and pointed it at me. Something heavy collided with my chest and tossed me backward, buffeting the air from my lungs. My feet scraped across the stone floor until I was pinned to the cave wall. High, cold laughter tore at my ears as I struggled against the unseen force. I could not move. "Fight me all you like. It makes no difference. I didn't teach you everything I know."

I screamed, feeding the fire that licked along my forearms with my rage, but I could not push it forward. Every time I tried, the edges of the blaze died away. "*Fel!*" I shouted, but even my Word of Power did not give me the strength to break free. Invisible hands grasped at my limbs, tugging me in all directions. My flames flickered and died as Mogra dragged me along the wall.

After another push cracked my head against the stone and sent stars spinning around my head, Mogra appeared to grow bored with me. "You are becoming an annoyance," she spat. She began to squeeze the air with her fingers, and my throat closed up, blocked by magic and fear.

"Ailynn!" Through my swimming gaze, I caught a glimpse of Raisa fighting wildly against Mogra's grip.

A startled look to crossed Mogra's face, and she lowered her hand. Air rushed back into my aching, starved lungs, but she did not even notice. Her attention remained focused on Raisa. "You can't possibly..." she muttered.

Raisa tried to pull away, but she froze when Mogra lifted her hand, allowing fresh flames to dance between her fingers. She stared into Raisa's eyes for a long moment, but her flames died away as her hand wandered down along the front of her body, tracing the line between her hipbones. The gesture infuriated me. I could not bear to watch Mogra touch Raisa for any reason.

"I thought so," she murmured, the dark amusement returning to her voice. "I was going to separate you from your precious Ailynn forever, but I think I will keep you together. It will be much more satisfying when she realizes." Finally, she turned back to me. I made one last attempt to free myself, but I was still stuck against the wall. "I have decided to let you keep your little whore after all." Mogra shoved Raisa away from her, and she ran toward me, clutching desperately at my arm. I could not move to pull her closer. "I cannot leave you here to disrupt my plans."

The fire died away from Mogra's hands, and her lips formed ancient Words, Words of Power she had never shared with me. They ran together like a song, and before I could move to defend myself, a howling noise exploded in my head. The ceiling above us cracked, and the sky split open at its seams.

Dust rained down on us from overhead, and wind tore at our clothes. Suddenly, we were flying up, up, up into the sky. Raisa's mouth opened in a scream, but the sound was lost in the cold air blasting across our faces and arms. She squeezed my hand, which had miraculously stayed in hers, and I squeezed back, unable to do anything else.

I turned my head down and saw an endless expanse of blue, broken by the occasional wisp of white cloud. I panicked and started to struggle away from Raisa, but she pulled me closer. 'Don't look,' she mouthed, keeping her eyes shut tight.

Too late. I followed Raisa's example and closed my eyes so I would not have to see how high up we were. If we were going to fall to our deaths, I did not want to watch. Slowly, the howling tongues of air licking at my skin and tearing my clothing like claws began to soften, drifting farther and farther away. I sank deeper into the darkness behind my closed eyelids. My tight grip of Raisa's hand never wavered.

* * *

I awoke next to a river, my face warmed by the sun. The grass was soft and comfortable, and I took in a slow breath through my nose, enjoying the sweet, earthy smell. I could not remember losing consciousness, but the aches all over my body told me I had probably fallen here. *Some adventurer and rescuer I am. This is the second time*

I've passed out now, first when I saw Cate in half-shape and again after that terrifying flight. The flight. *Raisa!*

I opened my eyes, breathing a sigh of relief when I saw Raisa's familiar form beside me. She did not seem to be hurt, and when I rested my head against her chest, I heard an even, steady heartbeat. Her eyes were closed, but her breathing seemed normal, and she did not appear to have any broken bones. Something must have cushioned our fall.

Slowly, I pulled myself up into a sitting position and looked around. We were in a beautiful clearing, but I did not recognize the trees around me. We were not in the forest of my childhood. A bright, clear river gurgled along beside me, and a little cottage was tucked away next to a bend in the stream.

"Where are we?" I whispered.

"Here, of course."

I had not been expecting an answer to my question, and I whirled around to see who had spoken. An old man in a simple brown tunic stood several feet behind me. His wild grey hair exploded around his head, and his face had the texture of old leather. Despite that, he was surprisingly tall and sturdily built. The scent of magic clung to him, and I knew he was a fellow *Ariada*. I cast a worried glance at Raisa, who had not yet opened her eyes, but the stranger made no move to harm either of us.

"Arim dei," he said.

Even though I was stunned by his sudden appearance, I returned the greeting. "Arim dei."

"It isn't every day that two lovely girls are falling into the middle of my back yard. No indeed, not every day."

"Well, it certainly wasn't a pleasant experience," I mumbled, not sure what else to say.

The old man laughed. His eyes crinkled at the corners, further reassuring me of his good intentions. "Of course it wasn't. If you're anything like your mother, air was never your favorite element. I'm rather surprised she had the control to summon such a great wind."

My eyes narrowed. "You know my mother?"

"Of course. You look just like her, you know."

I shuddered at the memory of Mogra's warped appearances. I hesitated to discuss the subject, but eventually decided I should make sure this stranger knew what Mogra was capable of. Although I doubted she would follow us, it was still a possibility. "Mogra is not the same anymore. She's dangerous and unpredictable. I don't even know why she sent us here."

"That's because she didn't," the man said. "I brought you here."

I frowned at him, confused. "What do you mean?"

"Mogra was trying to send you to the timeless sands of the Old Desert. I stopped the great wind and called it here instead."

My eyes widened. The Old Desert bordered the southwestern corner of Amendyr, just beneath Liarre territory. Much like the forest, it was so large and well known that it did not need an official name, although many colorful descriptions were often attached to it. If Raisa and I had landed there, we surely would have starved.

The stranger seemed to sense my nervousness, because he said, "Don't worry, Ailynn. You are safe here."

Questions swirled in my head, almost reminding me of the wind that had carried us here. I studied the strange old man, trying to remember if I had ever met him when I was very small. No memories came to the surface. "How do you know my name? Do you know my mother?"

"I loved her once," he said, and his features darkened. "Many, many years ago. But she would not have me. She would not have anyone. Mogra was a great woman. It's painful to watch her being consumed by the darkness." He noticed the surprised, almost pained expression on my face and gave me a sympathetic look. "The fault is not all hers, though. Mogra's only sin was greed. That was the doorway through which the darkness entered and overpowered her."

"I have no idea what you are talking about," I admitted, but paused when I felt a cool shadow pass overhead and looked up into the sky. Dark clouds drifted in front of the sun, blocking it from view. I sensed the loss of warmth and gave Raisa another worried glance. She made a soft groaning noise and began to stir. I slid one of my arms beneath her shoulders. "Will you please help me take her inside?" I asked, gesturing at the cottage. "I assume you live there."

"Of course," he said. "I won't leave you two out in the rain."

At last, Raisa opened her eyes. "Rain?" she asked, stumbling over the word as though it tasted strange in her mouth. "Oh, Ailynn, you're here. I knew you wouldn't leave me again."

I smiled down at her, relieved she was all right. "Yes, I'm here. Let me help you inside." I pulled us onto our feet. She grimaced, probably feeling just as battered and bruised as I did. The old man reached out to help steady us both, and the strength of his grip surprised me.

Raisa accepted his help. "Thank you, sir, I hope you don't consider me rude for asking, but who are you, exactly?"

"Sometimes I hardly remember my own name nowadays, but it's Doran. Now, follow me." With those words, we hurried through the light drizzle of rain and into the little cottage.

CHAPTER EIGHT

"THANK YOU FOR TAKING us in," I said as Doran passed me a fresh cup of tea. I held the mug tight, grateful for the warmth. Although we had avoided the worst of the rain, riding the great wind had left me with a chill I could not seem to escape.

"You are most welcome."

Doran set a mug of tea in front of Raisa as well, and she gave him a smile. I shifted closer to her, trying to share body heat. "We are both very grateful," I said, including her in my thanks. "I promise that we won't intrude for more than a day. I don't want to strain your hospitality."

Doran shook his head and took the remaining empty seat at the table. "You will need to stay for longer than that, Ailynn."

His answer surprised me, and I set my cup back down on the table. "I will? Why?"

"If you are going to face Mogra, you must learn to defend yourself. Your fire might be enough to protect you from ordinary threats, but Mogra knows all of the same tricks you do. You have to fight her with something she is not expecting. Before you leave, I'm going to teach you battle magic."

A worried look crossed Raisa's face, but she lifted her tea to hide it. I did not blame her for being afraid. Battle magic was an incredibly difficult discipline, and it required an intense amount of mental focus. One small mistake, and even an experienced *Ariada* could find themselves harmed by their own Words of Power. I gave Doran a long look. I had sensed he was an *Ariada* seconds after meeting him, and although he was old, I could catch glimpses of the power he must have held in his youth. It did not surprise me that he knew battle magic.

"What do you intend to teach me?"

"If Mogra was your teacher, I'm sure she covered offensive battle magic already." He gazed around the small hut, and his eyes flicked toward the kitchen fireplace. "You could probably feed that fire enough to burn down my house in less than a minute. But there is more to being a witch than brute strength. I will teach you how to protect your mind as well as your body."

I recalled how easily Mogra had immobilized me in Raisa's cave, and my lips twisted into a frown. The last time I had felt that helpless, she had drugged my tea and stolen Raisa away. I would not allow her to manipulate me again. I stood and bowed my head. "Thank you. If you are willing to share your knowledge with me, I am eager to learn."

"It's decided, then. We'll start in the morning. Once you've shown enough progress, I think it would be a good idea for you to find Cate." I was surprised that Doran knew Cate, but I shouldn't have been. If he was an enemy of Mogra's, he was probably a friend to the rebellion. Perhaps Cate had even told him we would fall from the sky and land his back yard. That must have been an interesting conversation.

Raisa turned to give me a questioning look. "Cate? Who is she?"

"A member of the rebellion," I explained. "She saved my life, and she's also the one you have to thank for your freedom. I couldn't have broken the spell without the book she gave me."

Raisa smiled. "If she is a friend of yours, then she is my friend as well. Besides, a camp full of fighters and *Ariada* sounds like a safe place to be if Mogra decides to come after us."

I stared at her. "Wait, you know what the rebellion is?" Trapped in the cave with no one but Mogra and a lustful nobleman's son to talk to, the fact that Raisa understood the current danger to the kingdom surprised me. I had not heard of the rebellion until I left the lonely forest and traveled out into the neighboring villages.

Raisa stared down into her tea. "Mogra told me. She was enthusiastic about the creations she made to hunt them down. I was the only person she could talk to."

"Perhaps that is a conversation better left for tomorrow," Doran said. "There is a mattress and blankets in the next room that you are welcome to share."

He got up from his chair, putting a hand to his lower back. I did not take the abrupt departure personally. Doran probably wanted to rest, especially after using his energy to redirect Mogra's magical wind.

Although his body was sturdily built despite his age, time had beaten it down.

"Sleep well, Ailynn," he added, looking at me. "You will need your strength."

* * *

When we finally retired for the night, Raisa and I shared the mattress Doran had left on the floor by the fireplace. "It feels so strange to be sleeping somewhere other than my bed," Raisa said quietly as we lay in each other's arms. "I can hardly believe I'm finally free."

I chuckled, hardly believing it myself. "But you believe the part about riding on a great wind and being saved by an old wizard?"

Raisa sighed and shifted closer. She frowned, and I smoothed out the worry lines that creased her forehead with my thumb. Guilt ate at me for teasing her. Staying in one room for that long was unimaginable to me. I had spent a lot of time in the cave as well, but at least I was able to leave at night. "Are you frightened? This is your first night away."

Raisa shook her head, and the soft strands of her hair tickled my shoulder. It had grown past her waist again since our reunion. "No. I am a little unsure of myself, but not afraid. I am glad to be free, but mostly glad to be with you again." Her whispered words warmed my cheeks and made my heart beat faster. "I will miss my books and my drawings, though. I wish I could have brought them with me."

Remembering the drawings made my eyes widen. It pleased me to know Raisa had missed me enough to draw so many pictures. Coming from her, they did not seem threatening or invasive, even the erotic ones. "Maybe your things are still there," I said, trying to offer her some comfort.

"I don't want to go back there, not even after Mogra's dead. I never want to see that place again. I can always purchase new books, and perhaps even write some of my own. And I can make new drawings." Her soft hand made contact with my side, rubbing in a slow circle. I shivered at the touch. "My drawings of you will be even better now that I have seen the real thing."

"You can draw anything you want," I said, kissing her forehead. My fingers traced a line along her hip. "I am sure that your new drawings will be beautiful. You are beautiful."

"I want to draw everything, but you are my favorite subject." The fire had almost burned to ash and embers, and so I was surprised when her lips found mine, but not unwilling. It soothed some of my hurt feelings to know that Raisa wanted to initiate contact.

Despite my better judgment, I let her leave a trail of kisses along my throat, sighing heavily against one of the blankets. When her hand slid under my shirt to caress the bare skin of my stomach, I flinched and pulled back.

"Stop," I said, gripping her wrist.

Even through the darkness, I could see the hurt in Raisa's eyes. She pulled her hand away and remained still beside me. The silence stretching between us made my chest ache. "We are guests in Doran's house," I mumbled at last. It was a pathetic excuse, but I could not bring myself to voice the true reason. My broken heart still needed more time to heal.

Raisa shifted on the mattress and turned away so her back faced me. Hurt settled on me, but since my rejection had caused her bad mood, I could not really complain. "I'm sorry," I whispered.

Raisa reached behind her, taking one of my arms and draping it over her waist. I felt a little better as I pressed against her warm back. "No, I'm sorry. I know I hurt you. I can't expect you to forgive me in one day."

Words began to build inside of me, but I did not know how to sort through all of them. I did want to make love with Raisa again, but I was afraid, not of the act itself, but of exposing all of my heart to her. Seeing her with Byron had nearly destroyed me, but beneath that ran a much deeper fear. I was terrified that once she saw into the depths of my soul, Raisa would think me a coward. Even though she had broken my heart, I was the one who did not feel worthy of her. She never would have needed to lie with Byron if I had not abandoned her in the first place.

"I love you," I murmured against her hair, not wanting to fall asleep without telling her.

Raisa squeezed my hand, tying our fingers together. "I love you, too," she said. Both of us closed our eyes and tried to find a few fitful hours of sleep.

* * *

I was back in the cave, pinned helplessly to the wall as Mogra held Raisa in her grip. Mogra's once-familiar face was warped, twisted almost beyond recognition. Her eyes narrowed with blazing hatred, but my own fire proved useless, trapped up in my breath. No matter how hard I tried to conjure my Words of Power, I could not force them out of my mouth.

"Ailynn!"

I stared into Raisa's terrified face, but I could do nothing. I was frozen in place. My lips could not even form her name. I could only watch in horror as Mogra's burning fingers wrapped around Raisa's throat and began to squeeze. Crimson flames licked at her pale skin, eating away at her flesh. Her screams of agony reminded me of the kerak. She burned away, crumbling to black ash.

I woke screaming, arms thrown out to both sides as I struggled with the blankets. "Ailynn? Ailynn!" I ignored the voice calling out to me, trying to push away clinging hands. Instead, the hard grip tightened, holding me down against a mattress. Breathing quickly, I pushed at the attacker's arms. When that failed, I went limp, trying to get my bearings.

Slowly, I became aware of soothing words and soft touches coming from beside me. Raisa. I relaxed and let her stroke my face and chest as she reassured herself that I was all right.

"Ailynn, dear heart, open your eyes."

I forced my eyes open. The fire had died in the hearth, and the room was almost completely dark. Still, the faint traces of starlight that seeped in through the windows illuminated Raisa just enough for me to make out her silhouette. She was hovering over me, concern rolling off her in waves. Even though I could not see her face, her touch and her voice told me everything.

"Stay with me," I gasped, surprised by the desperate, breathy quality of my own words. I had not chosen to say them.

"Always."

That one word was all I needed to hear. My heartbeat slowed down, my breathing grew even and deep, and I drifted into a much more peaceful sleep. For now, I believed her. We would not be parted again.

CHAPTER NINE

"NO, CONCENTRATE HARDER."

I groaned, resting my hands on my knees and bending down to catch my breath. Doran had summoned me outside the cottage after lunch, and even though the sun still hung stubbornly in the sky, I was already exhausted. For an old man, Doran had a surprising amount of focus and stamina. Biting back a plea for mercy, I straightened and prepared for another assault.

I was supposed to be learning how to shield myself against magical attacks. The technique involved pulling the air around me into a physical barrier, but I had never whispered with air the way I did with fire, and it was difficult to react fast enough to Doran's attacks. The Word of Power Doran had taught me complicated things, *Secutem* from the ancient word for shield. Theoretically, if I spoke the word while performing the magical action, the two would become linked in my mind, acting as a trigger to help me to perform the spell faster. But theory was different than practice, and I had not bothered learning any new Words of Power for the past several years.

"Again," Doran shouted. A moment later, a powerful blast of wind came flying at me.

I threw up my arms. *"Secutem!"* The word did me little good. Doran pushed me backwards and I nearly tripped. It took me several moments to regain my footing. I swiped my damp forehead with the back of my hand, trying to clear the sweat and loose hair from my eyes. My hair tie was doing me little good with all of the air blowing around my head.

"Sorry," I panted. "I'm finding it difficult to close all of the holes." While constructing a barrier was relatively simple if I had time to think about it, it was much harder to cover my entire body with only a few seconds notice. In a real fight, I knew I would not get that much warning.

"Protect your chest and head first," Doran said. "They're the most important. Better to lose a few fingers than your face."

I scowled, pressing my lips together in frustration. I did not like the idea of leaving any part of me unprotected, but he was right. It would be quicker and easier to block the center of my body instead of worrying so much about the extremities.

"Again," said Doran.

This time, I gave the threads of air surrounding me a solid tug, yanking them together in time to create an admirable shield. As I pulled at the magical energy, I repeated the word *"Secutem!"* Unfortunately, Doran's bolt of energy was aimed at my knees this time, and I fell forward onto the ground. I found myself staring up at the sky, rubbing my aching head. So much for that.

"Here," he said, offering me his hand. I took it, gratefully accepting his help. His old age and feeble appearance certainly belied his power. I was soundly defeated for at least the twentieth time that day. "Don't worry, that shield was a good one. It just wasn't in the right place."

I groaned, giving my head a brief shake to try and clear away the blurriness at the edges of my vision. "A good shield in the wrong place isn't very helpful."

"You will learn."

I was already learning a lot from Doran. I just wished the lessons did not always involve so many bruises. By the time we were done, my muscles shook with exertion and my head swam. The harmless looking old man had used wind to blow me off balance, lobbed balls of fire at me, and even cracked the earth directly beneath my feet. I had several scratches, bruises, and even a few burns along my upper arm, several from my own fire.

"Better," Doran said at last, giving me a smile. "We will continue your training tomorrow."

Despite my exhaustion, a warm glow of pride grew in my chest. I had managed to deflect a few of Doran's attacks near the end, although I was sure I looked the worse for wear.

"Ailynn, by the Maker, what happened to you?" a familiar voice called from behind me. Raisa peeked out of the front door, staring at my disheveled appearance.

I flinched at the panic in her voice, but Doran laughed as he gently pushed her to one side and entered the house. "Isn't it obvious? She missed."

Raisa glanced from Doran back to me, looking bewildered. "He did that to you?" She gestured at the burns on my shoulder and the streaks of dirt that covered my face and clothes.

"Trust me," I muttered. "He is much more dangerous than he looks."

"It looks like I need to take care of you," Raisa cupped my cheeks in her hands. "Come inside and let me help you clean up."

I willingly accepted Raisa's assistance. "Who am I to reject an offer of help from such a beautiful woman?" I teased, managing a tired smile.

Enjoying the warmth of Raisa's hand around mine, I allowed her to lead me inside. Doran had retreated to his bedroom, and I suspected he was eager to get some rest.

"Stay here," she said, seating me at the table.

I closed my eyes, sighing happily as I leaned my weight against the back of the wooden chair. It was sturdy and well balanced. It felt wonderful to sit down and rest my aching back.

A few minutes later, Raisa returned with some hot water and a cloth, which she used to clean my face and the raw pink flesh on my arm. I relaxed, enjoying the pampering without protest. Once most of the dirt had been wiped away, she pressed against my side. "Here, let me get you some new clothes."

Raisa shifted against me and I noticed something. The feel of Raisa's body, even while seated, seemed different. Perhaps I had been too distracted to notice it before, but now that we were relatively safe, it leapt to the forefront of my mind. Curious, I stood up and pulled her into my arms. She did not object, staring silently at me as she wrapped her own arms around my waist. Despite the newness of our physical relationship, we had shared a bed for years before that. I knew how her body fit against mine. Her breasts were fuller, her lower abdomen swelling out into a soft, womanly curve. Suddenly, Mogra's strange behavior in the cave made sense. She was with child.

I shrugged out of her embrace, ignoring her protests. She reached for me, but I backed away. "Why didn't you tell me?" I demanded, pointing at her stomach. Only a keen or experienced eye would have noticed, but I had watched Mogra treat several women at various stages of pregnancy. I had even taken care of a few myself after I inherited her practice. I felt like a fool for taking so long to notice.

Realizing what had caused my reaction, Raisa frowned and looked away. When she did not offer an explanation, I continued. "You lied to me. You hid this from me."

"You have only been back for a few days," Raisa said, glancing back at me. "Exactly when was I supposed to tell you? The moment you came through my door after a year apart?"

Remembering Raisa and Byron together cut me even deeper. Surely he was the father. The thought made my stomach lurch. "I can't. I don't," I stuttered, overwhelmed.

"Just listen to me for one moment," said Raisa, her words coming out in a rush. "Then you may be as angry as you like. The Maker knows your feelings are justified." I nodded. I did not know what else to say anyway.

"I knew this might happen when I made the choice to be with Byron. It was a calculated risk. This doesn't change how I feel about you, but I won't blame you if it changes how you feel about me. I was going to tell you once I figured out the best way. When I realized that I was..." Her voice cracked. "When I was expecting, I pretended the child was yours." She spoke the last sentence in a quiet whisper that broke my heart all over again.

I looked away from her, unable to witness the pain her eyes. So many emotions stormed inside of me I could scarcely rein them in. I had to leave. Anywhere would be better than standing here, frozen, while Raisa stared at me with tears in her eyes. "I'm going back outside," I said stiffly, taking a quick step back.

Raisa flinched at the rejection, but did not try and stop me. "If you need me—"

"I will find you," I mumbled. Part of me wanted to tell her I loved her before I left, but I could not bring myself to say the words. Turning away, I wandered out of the front door, only glancing over my shoulder once. Raisa's face was buried in her hands, her shoulders shaking.

Outside, the sunny weather was an irritating contrast to my dark and gray mood. I sat by the river, trailing a finger loosely in the water. Despite how angry I was, the last thing Raisa had revealed echoed in my ears. '*I pretended that the child was yours.*' She really did love me in spite of how much pain she had caused. She loved me enough to want children with me. If only the child were mine. Now, if I stayed with her, it would be impossible to erase the memory of Byron from our lives. I didn't know if I could forgive her.

Staring down into the water, I caught a glimpse of my own heartbroken expression. It reminded me of Raisa's. I splashed the image away with my hand. Anger boiled within me, directed at Raisa, but also at myself. I had already abandoned her once. Could I survive another separation?

I wanted someone to blame for my pain, but as tempting as it was to put all of the responsibility on Raisa's shoulders, I could not forget my own complicity. Both of us had made painful choices. I had left her trapped and alone without even saying a proper goodbye. She had tried to secure her freedom using the only means available to her. She had made a choice—a choice that hurt me deeply—but so had I. I needed to accept that if I wanted to stay with her.

Children had never been a part of the future I had dreamed of with Raisa. Never in my future at all. But, now the image surfaced in my mind. Raisa watching as the child leapt into my arms. Mogra surfaced, too. My own mother was certainly not the best role model to follow. I was already considering the best way to raise the child, and that surprised me. I did not remember choosing to act as a second parent. Perhaps there was no decision to make. I sighed. Being with Raisa meant accepting her child. Perhaps this was my punishment for abandoning her when she needed my protection. Immediately, I felt guilty for viewing the unborn child as a punishment. None of this was its fault.

A feeling of helplessness crashed over me. I felt like I was drowning, gasping for breath. Would Raisa have been better off without me? Would I have been better off without her? But we had both waited too long to throw away what we had. I owed it to her and myself to try. The only other option I had was to leave Raisa, and just thinking about it made my heart ache twice as much. I sighed and stood up, leaving the brook behind. I had promised her I would try, and I would keep that promise. I had already broken so many others.

Rae D. Magdon

CHAPTER TEN

ALTHOUGH I RETURNED TO the cottage, I did not speak to Raisa for the rest of the day. She respected my need for space. Instead, she cast glances in my direction whenever I passed close to her. We ate in silence, but I forced myself to share the table with her anyway, unwilling to widen the rift between us. Raisa seemed grateful for the small concession.

Climbing into bed with her that night, the wall between us finally crashed down. I had considered taking a blanket and settling on the floor somewhere, or even going back outside, but images of Raisa sleeping alone, curled into a tight ball, prevented me from leaving. We had spent over a year sleeping apart from each other. I would not waste another night.

Raisa gave me a cautious look when I joined her on the mattress. She did not move to touch me, but she did give me a warm smile. I was the one who finally made contact, curling an arm over her hip and pulling her against my side. Her muscles tightened briefly before she melted into me. Our bodies fit together, two halves reunited. Even the curve of her belly matched the shape of my side. The physical reminder of her pregnancy made me flinch, and Raisa froze.

I propped myself up on one elbow and touched her shoulder, urging her to look up at me. Behind the fear, sadness, and loneliness in her expression, I saw love. Despite everything, I still loved her, too. I was not ready to forgive her, or even ready to say it, but I could not let the distance between us continue to grow. I bent my head and caught her lips in a kiss. Raisa whimpered at the sudden contact, understanding and accepting what I was asking for. There was no slow burn, no torturous anticipation, only need.

Once I initiated, Raisa did not wait. She made soft noises of impatience against my lips, and her hands roamed along my sides, trying to pull me closer. Her touch made my skin heat up beneath my shirt, but I was not ready to allow her such freedom. I began to remove her dress instead, tugging at the stubbornly tight laces in between kisses. They were difficult to untangle in the dark, and when I failed to untie them fast enough, she reached down to help me. With her help, they came loose at last. I gasped as the neckline of her dress slid down to reveal the pale skin of her shoulders.

I tugged the loosened fabric the rest of the way down her arms, craving more of her skin. She drew in a sharp breath, and the tips of her breasts hardened. I circled them with my thumbs, amazed at how quickly her body responded to my touch. Dizzy with want, I nipped at a soft place just beneath her jaw, leaving a mark along her pale skin. Her pulse sped up, but she did not try to stop me, tilting her chin instead and granting me even more access.

I left more red marks along the soft column of her throat, across her collarbone and down her chest, trying to burn my presence into her skin with teeth, lips, and tongue. I wanted everyone who saw her to know that she was mine. I listened to the cadence of her breathing, careful to back away when the rhythm came too quickly. My mouth finally reached her breasts and she forgot her caution. She wrapped her arms around me, stroking over my back in gentle circles. "Ailynn, please."

Too impatient to wait any longer, I pushed the dress the rest of the way down, dragging it over her hips and leaving it tangled around her knees. My hand crept lower, pausing briefly at her stomach, exploring its unfamiliar shape. Raisa's lips parted, but I silenced her with a kiss. Whatever she wanted to say, I was not in the mood to listen. I wanted to talk with our bodies.

My hand wandered down along her abdomen, pausing there for a moment before cupping firmly between her legs. She was all warm skin and liquid silk, and I groaned at the wetness spilling over my fingertips. I drank in her shallow breaths, savoring the rapid thud of her heartbeat as I pulled the hard point of her breast between my lips. While everything else threatened to fall apart, this connection between us was undeniable.

I slid inside of her gently at first, and then with more force as her thighs parted for me. She gasped and adjusted the angle of her hips, pushing down to meet my thrust. I was caught for a moment before her muscles accepted my touch and relaxed. I released her nipple and stared up through the darkness, searching for her eyes. "Please," I breathed against her skin, remembering what she had said the first time we had done this. "Please tell me you're still mine."

"I'm yours, Ailynn," Raisa whispered. "I always have been."

I began moving deep within her, curling forward to catch against the full place along her front wall. Soft cries escaped from between her parted lips with every push of my hand, and I caught them all in a deep kiss. My chest could have been gaping open, the way she saw into my heart, but I kept my focus on the hand working steadily between her thighs. I skated over the swollen bud above her entrance again and again, enjoying the way it made her tense and sigh. She shuddered in my arms, but I only held her tighter. The first time I had taken Raisa, I had taken her in anger. Now, I took her in desperation, unable to hide or suppress the storm of emotions between us. I needed her. I craved her like water and air. Not just physically, but spiritually. I needed her to need me.

I felt a strange mixture of satisfaction and sadness when her body seized up, and her muscles locked tight as she whispered my name. Her voice broke in a strangled sob, and a rush of heat poured over my palm. I tried to push my fingers deeper, but her muscles squeezed down so tight I could scarcely move. The hard point beneath my thumb began to throb, but I kept stroking over its tip, determined to extend her pleasure for as long as possible. It was not until she went completely limp beneath me and I noticed the tears rolling down her cheeks that I eased my hand away.

She tucked her face in my shoulder, and her teardrops slid against my skin. I rocked her gently, murmuring words in her ear that neither of us would remember later, holding her tight against my chest. My heart's wounds began to heal. Raisa still loved me, still wanted me. She spoke in a soft, hoarse voice I could barely hear. "I understand if you want to leave, but please, please don't."

"I'm here," I told her, pressing kisses into her hair. I tried to promise that I would not leave, but the words refused to come.

"Ailynn, do you trust me?" she asked, gazing into my eyes.

I tried to look away, but her hand cupped my cheek, holding me in place. The touch of her palm burned, and heat crept over my cheeks. "I trust you," I said, but the words caught in my dry throat. Did I trust Raisa? Could I trust her not to hurt me again? She had already caused me so much pain, and she had the potential to cause me so much more.

Raisa shook her head, blonde strands of her hair catching the firelight. "Please, Ailynn. I know I'm not worthy of your trust now. All I ask is the chance to earn it back. I hate seeing you in so much pain."

"I'm not in pain," I lied.

"Then why won't you let me make love to you?" I could not answer her question. After a long, tense moment of silence, she pulled away from my embrace. "I'm sorry. I shouldn't have asked. After what I've done, you have every right to hate me."

"Raisa, I could never hate you."

"I have promised over and over again that I only love you, only want you. What else can I do to convince you?"

I stared past her face, looking out into the darkness of the room. Raisa's hand drifted down from my cheek to rest on my shoulder, still warm against my skin. "I just..." I could not finish the sentence. After everything I had done to be with Raisa, was I going to deny myself now because of my fears? Yes, Raisa might hurt me again, but the broken bond between us hurt more. I wanted to repair it.

I dissolved in her arms, letting our bodies come back together. She was slow and patient with me, covering my face with light butterfly kisses that flared like fire sparks against my skin. Finally, her lips met mine. How did she always know just what I wanted? For a moment, I allowed myself to be overwhelmed by the warmth and sweetness of Raisa's kiss. But the kiss was not enough. I wanted another. Our mouths fought, struggling for control, but I knew I would let Raisa win this time. My teeth scraped her lower lip, and she hissed against my mouth as her hands wandered down my back, pulling me close.

Her gentle palms explored the strip of flesh between my pants and shirt as I curled my fingers in her hair. The contact stopped, and I cried out in a soft protest. I tried to tilt her back onto the mattress, but she resisted and remained balanced over me. "No. It's my turn. I have been very patient." She removed my hand from the back of her neck and placed our joined fingers over my stomach, holding her breath as she waited to see if her touch was welcome.

I sighed, forcing my body to go limp and stretching my arms above my head. If Raisa wanted to be with me despite everything, how could I say no? "I trust you," I whispered, swallowing down the nervous knot in my throat.

Raisa smiled. Reverently, lovingly, she helped me out of my shirt, pulling it over my head and past my outstretched arms. Her eyes raked up and down my bare torso. I shivered under her heated gaze. "Ailynn," she murmured, placing a line of quick kisses along my shoulder. Her fingers traced curious patterns against my sides, stroking up from my hips and caressing my ribs. "Let me make love to you. You are so beautiful."

My eyes drifted shut as she palmed my breasts, and a low, satisfied groan vibrated in my throat. The noise seemed unnaturally loud to my ears, but I did not have time to be embarrassed. Raisa trapped the hardened tips of my breasts between her fingers, coaxing even more soft sounds of pleasure from me. When I realized I could not stifle them, I stopped trying.

I tugged at my pants, pulling them off and leaving the rest of my clothes on the floor. Her half-lidded gaze traveled up the line of my legs, and her eyes felt like two small circles of flame crawling over my skin. I trembled as they settled at the juncture of my thighs. As her fingertips moved lower, it took me several moments to catch my breath and still the rapid beating of my heart.

The first touch was cautious, barely brushing my hip. The second touch trailed down the line of my thigh. She coaxed my knees apart, and, as she settled between my legs, her mouth, too, moved lower. I clutched the mattress, trembling as she took the sensitive tip of my breast between her lips. The blissful warmth took me by surprise, and my hips bucked forward, but it only lasted a moment.

Raisa continued her downward path, easing one of my legs over her shoulder and settling on her stomach. I froze, torn between fear and anticipation, but she went lower than I expected. Slowly, achingly, she ran the tip of her tongue along my inner thigh. My fear became want, and I reached down to grasp one of her shoulders. "Please." Once she had me pleading for her touch instead of just enduring it, Raisa seemed satisfied. She urged my legs even further apart and dipped her head.

The sweet burn of her mouth made me flinch at first. It was unfamiliar, almost too intense, and it took me several moments to process the sensations. I struggled to separate the softness of her lips, the heated silk of her mouth, the rolling glide of her tongue. Although her motions were gentle, it felt as though she was devouring me whole. The muscles of my stomach trembled. Each soft pull, each flutter left me gasping for air. I groped forward, moving my hand from her shoulder to the back of her head in a desperate attempt to pull her closer.

Raisa seemed to know my body better than I did. While I lay panting beneath her, unable to form even the shape of her name with my lips, she began a thorough exploration. It only took her a few moments to discover a circular stroke that made my back arch. Once she found it, she repeated it again and again. The warmth of her tongue drew an answering warmth from inside me, and she had me rocking forward in search of more within the space of a few heartbeats.

She never remained in one place for long. Whenever the heavy, throbbing pressure along the swollen bud became too much, she darted down to my opening instead, teasing the shivering muscles there. I could not choose one over the other, and although I kept a tight grip on the back of her head, I could not find the strength to direct her mouth. Every brush of her lips brought with it a blaze of need, and each flick of her tongue had me fearing I would burst into flames.

One last stroke, and I was lost to another world. My head fell back as waves of bliss broke over me. My hips lifted to follow Raisa's mouth. I tangled my fingers deeper in her hair, pulling her tighter against me. The unbearable ache inside of me finally released, and sharp pulses of wetness spilled out with each shuddering ripple. Only one thought pierced the fog that filled my head. Why had I waited so long for this?

I slowly came back to myself and Raisa was still resting between my legs. She released the seal of her lips and pressed sweet kisses over the twitching tip of my clit, easing me through the aftershocks. I let my hand fall away from her head and stared down at her in wonder. My own attempts at self-pleasure were nothing like what I had just experienced, and even the orgasm I had stolen during our first time together could not compare. "That was...I can't find the words."

Raisa shifted against me, resting her cheek against my belly and grinning up at me. "It's a start," she said. "I think both of us need a little more practice."

It took me several moments to gather enough energy to respond. She had taken everything I had to give. "Later," I yawned, reaching down to pull her back up along my body. I flung my arm around her and drew her as close as I could.

"As long as there is a later," she whispered beside my ear. Her voice was the last thing I heard before I fell asleep.

PART THREE

Taken from the verbal accounts of Ailynn Gothel, Recorded and summarized by Lady Eleanor Kingsclere, née Sandleford

CHAPTER ONE

DESPITE OUR FRANTIC RECONNECTION the night before, numbness settled over me the next morning. My heart no longer ached with every breath, but Raisa and I had only taken the first steps toward repairing our broken bond. I woke before she did, trying to slip from her embrace without disturbing her. Raisa just held on tighter. I settled back down and buried my face in her hair.

"Good morning, my love," Raisa murmured, trailing her fingers along my back. She did not want to release me.

"Arim dei," I said, unable to keep a yawn from my voice.

Raisa smiled. "I'm glad you're still here."

"Did you think I wouldn't be?" I asked, hurt by the edge of surprise in her voice.

"I didn't mean it that way. I used to dream about moments like this, lying beside you after making love, but then I would always wake up. It's still a little difficult for me to believe that this is really happening."

"I'm sorry," I mumbled. "I don't know what I thought you meant. I guess I still feel guilty for leaving you in the first place."

I stared into Raisa's eyes, Cate's advice drifted through my mind. *'Nothing can guarantee happiness, Ailynn, even a soul mate. You must seek it within yourself.'* She had been right all along. Deep down, I had hoped all of my problems would vanish once we were reunited. Instead, they had only grown bigger. But despite everything we had endured, I was not ready to give up. "I know I have no right to place demands on you," I whispered. "But I want to know where we stand. What happens now?"

She sat up on the mattress. "I think that depends on you." Although she spoke clearly, I sensed Raisa's nervous energy. She curved a protective arm around her stomach, curling her knees closer to her body. "You know everything now. Does it change things between us?"

I did not have to search long for my answer. I still loved Raisa, child or no child. Unable to bear it any more, I clung to her naked form, praying I could banish some of the pain. I tucked my head over the soft swell of her shoulder, feeling her heartbeat against my chest. "Leaving you once almost broke me. I don't think I can do it again."

"Good." Raisa's voice broke, and a shudder rippled through her. "I'm not strong enough to lose you again."

"I'm here, aren't I?" Carefully, I reached a hand between our bodies and let it rest on her stomach. It already felt larger to me. How had I had missed such an obvious change? "Can you feel him moving yet?" I asked. I wanted to let her know I did not hate the child for driving a wedge between us, no matter how much I hated his father.

"Not yet." She clasped her hand over mine, letting our fingers weave together. "How do you know it will be a boy?"

"I don't know," I replied. "I just didn't want to call him an 'it.'"

The brilliant smile on Raisa's face reassured me I had made the right decision. "Do you want a son, Ailynn?"

Her use of the word 'son' made my heartbeat spike. "I'm not sure," I said, trying to disguise my fear. "I never thought about children much before."

"As long as you are with me, I will be happy."

"And I will be happy after the two of you find some clothes to wear," Doran called out from across the room. He exited his bedroom, holding his hand over his eyes.

Raisa squeaked and pulled the blanket up to her chin, blushing redder than a spring rose. I forced my own blush down and swallowed to ease the dryness in my throat. "Sorry, we were just changing."

"Changing into what?" Doran asked. He pointed at the floor beside the mattress. "From what little I saw, it looks like your clothes are done for."

I stared at Raisa's torn dress and my ruined shirt. They had been in bad shape before, but it was little more than a scrap now. "I don't suppose I could borrow a shirt?" I asked. "Mogra didn't exactly give us a chance to pack before we left."

"I'm sure I can find something suitable," Doran said. "Give me a moment." He retreated back into his bedroom.

As soon as he disappeared from sight, Raisa let out a heavy breath. "How long do you think he was standing there? And how long did we sleep, for that matter? The sun is already coming in through the window."

She was right. Beams of light streamed in through the clear glass and cast soft, glowing patterns on the cottage floor. "I don't know what time it is," I confessed, unable to resist trailing my fingers over her warm cheeks. Her embarrassment had left them flushed, and she caught my knuckles with her lips when they wandered too close. The warmth of her mouth made me forget about Doran's embarrassing interruption, and my skin burned for a different reason.

Raisa gave my hand one last kiss before drawing back again. "It could have been worse, and, honestly, I'm glad to be out of that dress." She kicked the crumpled fabric away from the mattress with a bare foot, letting it slide several inches across the floor. "It was getting too tight anyway."

"Have you thought of a name?" I asked, stroking her stomach. She let her eyes drift shut, purring in the back of her throat and pushing in to the touch. My feelings of heartbreak and betrayal would not disappear overnight, but I discovered the idea of a baby was also a little exciting. I found myself hoping the child would look exactly like her.

"No, not yet," she said without opening her eyes.

"Maybe I could—" Something large and soft landed on my face. I swatted away the fabric and realized Doran had thrown a fresh tunic and a pair of leggings on top of my head. "Thank you," I called out, shoving my arms through the tunic's sleeves and pulling it over my head.

Raisa had also been given clothes to wear, although I noticed that Doran had placed them next to her instead of dumping them on top of her head. "Stop frowning, Ailynn," she said. "I would rather see you smile."

Even tangled in the large shirt, I could not deny her such a simple request. I smiled as I poked my head through the open neck. I could give her a smile, at least. "Very well, if you insist."

Once we were awake and dressed, the hours flew by. After cooking, eating, and washing the dishes, we started cleaning the house. In an attempt to further my magical training, Doran declared that I was not permitted to use a ladder to clear away the cobwebs. After several unsuccessful attempts at summoning a controlled gust of air, I only succeeded in showering our heads with dust and knocking over a large stack of plates in the kitchen. Learning control of the other elements was much more difficult than it seemed. They would clearly not be mastered in a day.

Later, Doran took me back outside, and I spent the rest of the afternoon trying to summon a shield. Raisa watched. I had improved, but not by much. While I could deflect the small pinecones and pebbles Doran threw, I was unable to stop his barrage of magical attacks. Deadly quick, they knocked me off my feet more often than not.

"You're still thinking too much, Ailynn," Doran said as I picked myself up for what must have been the tenth time. "The entire purpose of a Word of Power is to prevent you from thinking. It's supposed to be instinctive."

"It doesn't feel instinctive."

"And that is why we practice, *Acha*." He drew his arm back, and I braced my feet on the ground in preparation.

"Secutem," I shouted, but I was already several seconds too late. The blast of air Doran sent my way bowled me over. I crashed to the ground with a painful thud, and by the time my head stopped spinning, Raisa had already risen from her seat. "Don't," I panted, holding up my hand in protest and clambering to my feet before she could reach me. "I'm fine."

Her forehead creased. "Are you sure? That one looked worse than usual."

"Didn't you see the backs of her leggings yesterday?" Doran asked. His grin showed even through the thick hairs of his beard. "The girl can take some punishment."

"I'll take that as a compliment," I muttered.

Doran seemed to sense my unease, because he closed the distance between us and put his hand on my shoulder. "Ailynn, controlling the elements with such precision usually takes years of study."

"But I don't have years," I protested. "Mogra could come after us tonight for all we know. What am I supposed to do?" Doran and Raisa had no answers, and frustrated, I bowed my head. "I wish making a shield felt as natural as my fire does. Maybe then I might stand a chance."

Doran remained silent for a long moment. "Perhaps we should try another method. You say that your fire feels natural to you?"

I lifted my chin and nodded. "Very natural. I've been summoning it since I was a child."

"Using what?"

"Anything handy. Grass and leaves, the sleeves of my clothes, the edges of my skin. All I need is something to burn, and air feeds the rest."

Doran let go of my shoulder and nudged the small of my back. "Try again. This time, use your fire to help you make your shield."

I gave him a doubtful look as I stepped back and brushed the dirt from my legs. "All right. It can't be any worse."

This time, when Doran drew back his arm, I was ready. *"Secutem!"*

Tongues of fire shot up from the blades of grass at my feet, sending plumes of smoke over my head. Instead of pushing out, I drew the blaze's energy in. The flames condensed, burning white-hot into a trembling wall, and a blast of scorching air rushed back toward my face. My vision swam with the heat, and it took me several seconds to realize I was still standing.

"Ailynn, put it out," Doran called over the top of the fire. I cut the flames off from the air they needed to feed, starving them until they receded back into the dirt. Once the wall had faded to embers, I crushed the smoldering remains beneath the sole of my boot. Raisa let out a joyful cry, and Doran smiled at me. "I would call that a success, *Acha*. If you need to light your shields on fire to make them work, so be it."

Exhaustion crashed over me and my shoulders sagged, but I smiled. "All the elements are connected, aren't they? I was using air to feed my fire all along. Maybe I can control it after all."

Doran nodded his head. "You would be surprised how few of our kind realize that. There is water in the earth we walk on, and air in the water we drink. Even fire has its place. If you learn how the elements are connected, you will be able to whisper with all of them. Now." He stepped back from the burnt patch of ground where I had summoned my shield. "Again."

CHAPTER TWO

BY THE TIME DORAN was finished with me, every muscle in my body screamed with pain, and I panted as I stumbled back toward the cottage. Raisa, on the other hand, remained cheerful and alert. After sitting in a cave with few ways to occupy her time, she found the change of scenery refreshing.

"Come on, Ailynn," she said as she came to join me. "How about we thank Doran for teaching you by making him a nice meal? It's getting too late to stay outside."

The sun had already disappeared behind the gently sloping hills, leaving behind orange streaks in the purples and blues of the night sky. The stars were still hidden, but the moon had already risen, surrounded by a pale grey ring. "You'll have no argument from me. I'm starved."

Lowering my gaze from the sky, I looked at the river that ran past the cottage. Other nighttime sounds already came from the trees, and so I was not too disturbed when I heard something rustling in the undergrowth behind Doran's house. I saw nothing unusual, but just as I was about to head inside, a flash of bright color caught the corner of my eye. I turned to look again. This time, two hovering, ghostly lights shone out at me from somewhere in the foliage. Surprised, I took a step back. The twin lights winked out. The back of my neck prickled in fear.

"Ailynn, are you all right? Your cheeks are flushed." I jumped, flinching at the touch of Raisa's hand on my shoulder.

I tried to reassure her with a smile. "I'm fine. I thought I saw something."

Before I could describe the ghostly, burning lights, Raisa's mouth fell open, her eyes widening as she stared at something over my shoulder. I turned to see a leering, distorted face peering at us out of the darkness, its peeling brown skin stretched tight over its skull. Two rows of pointed gray fangs appeared behind its curled back lips and two shining, yellow eyes stared back at us.

Raisa's scream startled me into action. I summoned my fire, drawing from the core of heat within me. Tongues of flame licked at my flesh, and the kerak let out a frightened shriek, drawing back into the undergrowth. Its glowing eyes winked out, and the blackness swallowed it up before I could send the blaze after it. I kept my arm raised, but it did not reappear.

"What was that?" Raisa stammered. Her fingers dug painfully into the side of my arm.

I frowned. "A kerak, I think." The creature had certainly looked similar, but the kerak I had seen before did not have eyes, only wide, gaping mouths. "Trust me. Whatever it was, we don't want to get close."

"Ailynn, Raisa, get inside," Doran shouted from behind us. "There must be more than one out there."

Raisa hurried in, and I kept staring out into the darkness just long enough to make sure she made it safely inside the cottage. I closed and bolted the door, letting the flames around my fingertips die down. "Will we be safe in here?"

Doran shook his head. "Not for long. That was just a scout. They have eyes for Mogra to use. More will come soon once they know where we are. We have to leave now." He hurried into the kitchen, yanking open drawers and rummaging through cupboards. He produced a pack from one of them and began filling it with as many supplies as he could reach. "Check inside the pantry, Ailynn. You'll find a supply of healing herbs there. Take whatever you can carry." I understood his meaning. If we were going up against Mogra's forces, we would certainly need them.

My eyes widened when I stepped into the pantry. For such a small space, it was surprisingly well stocked. Doran and my mother had more in common than I had anticipated. I scrambled to sort through the pouches and jars, trying to decide which would be most useful. I settled on a jar along the top shelf, and pulled it down to read its label. Cramproot would act as a muscle relaxant if any of us were injured or Raisa had problems with the baby. I shoved it into the pocket of my tunic, along with a generous supply of belladonna, aconite, and valerian root.

Once I found the herbs, I looked for the materials needed to clean and dress wounds. Doran's cupboards were organized, despite the almost haphazard appearance of the rest of the house. After I finished gathering what I needed, I stepped back out into the kitchen. Raisa waited for me with a pack slung over her shoulders. "I have no idea why Doran has clothes that fit us, but I managed to grab some. Here." She held open the front of the bag and allowed me to put my supplies inside.

"Where did Doran go?" I glanced around the kitchen.

"I'm not sure. Once I started helping with the food, he left."

I frowned. We already had food, clothes, and herbs, and our time was running out. What could the old wizard possibly be looking for? Moments later, he returned to the kitchen carrying a bunch of blue fabric in his arms. Gripped in his fingers was a little black comb.

"Here," he said, offering it to Raisa. She took the comb from him. I could feel its warmth radiating outward even from a distance, and I knew it had to be enchanted.

"Don't use it unless you need it," Doran said, confirming my suspicions. "If you find yourself in danger, throw it over your shoulder. It will protect you."

"Thank you," Raisa said. She tucked the comb into the bag along with the rest of our supplies.

"Take this one, too." He held a second comb, the same size and shape as the first. This one was brown instead of black and made of smooth, polished wood.

Raisa gave a nervous laugh and placed it in the pack along with the first. "Well, at least my hair should be manageable now." I was not sure whether to scold her or praise her for joking while the kerak still lurked outside, but it did make the knot of fear in my chest loosen a little.

"This is the last thing," Doran said, handing Raisa the blue fabric. It was a scarf. A plain looking thing, but well made. "Keep this close to you."

Since there was no longer very much room in the pack, Raisa wrapped it around her neck instead. "Where did you get this, Doran?" she asked as she caressed the threads. "Are you an enchanter as well as a wizard?"

"No. This is an old gift from a friend, but I sense you need it more than me."

"Thank you," she whispered, bowing her head.

"Don't use that one until the last possible moment. It is a last resort."

"I promise," she said. I hoped the time to use the gifts would never come. If we were lucky, we would never find out what hidden powers of protection they carried.

Before I could ask about the objects, the front door shuddered on its hinges. Outside, something pounded against it with a good deal of force. Raisa flinched, and Doran hurried toward the fireplace. "Here," he said, shoving a torch back into her hands. "You might need this."

Raisa eyed the torch, but Doran had already summoned a small globe of light in his hand. He lit its tip, and the wrappings caught fire. "They're made of ash," I told her. "If one of them gets to close, burn it." Raisa's eyes widened, but she tightened her grip on the torch and nodded.

Doran shared a glance with me, and I fed my own flames, letting the heat blaze around my clenched fists. If the kerak came, I would not let them pass. As one, we turned toward the door. With a sharp crack, the wood began to splinter, buckling against its frame. Finally, a crack appeared in the center, followed by slivers of pulp as the kerak tore through the wood. Its face peered through, black lips peeled over the roots of its teeth, and its glowing eyes fixed on me.

"Fel!" I flung out my hand, and a ball of fire spat from my open palm. It screamed toward the door, sparks dripping from its tail. The kerak screeched, trying to twist its body back through the hole. As soon as the flames made contact, its entire body ignited, skin sloughing off and crumbling away to dust. Howling came from outside, and the door fell to pieces, revealing several more dark, lanky figures on the front porch. Their scythe-like claws pulled back and prepared to swing.

"A shame," Doran said as he raised his crackling fists. "Remodeling this place is going to be expensive." The group of kerak lunged forward, but he was faster. Fire flashed from his fingertips, lashing out like the tail of a whip and curling around the nearest one's chest. It howled in agony as the blaze crawled over its body, scattering flakes of ash across the floor.

The other kerak drew back, hissing, but their caution did not last long. They began loping toward us again on uneven limbs, crossing the entryway and pouring into the kitchen. Together, Doran and I burned through as many of the monsters as we could reach. My tongue blazed with the bite of magic as I spoke my Word of Power again and again, sending bolts of fire streaking through the cottage. The kerak fell as soon as my flames touched them, but they came in endless waves. As soon as one crumbled, another took its place.

A scream came from behind me, and I whirled around to see Raisa driving her torch into another kerak's chest. The flames ate through its body, and its claws crumbled away inches from her throat. "We have to run," she shouted above the angry shrieks. "There are too many of them."

My eyes darted around the kitchen, trying to find a way out, but we were surrounded. The kerak had formed a line between us and the door. There was no other option. We would have to go through them. I threw both of my hands forward and up, but instead of aiming at the kerak, I pointed them toward the door. *"Secutem!"* Twin walls of blue fire rose up from the floorboards, spitting and popping wildly, stretching toward the ceiling. The kerak caught in the blaze howled. "Run!"

The three of us followed the burning path I had made, sprinting toward the door. Doran sent the kerak in front of us into the burning walls with a sweeping gust of air. They exploded in a shower of dust. Soon, we burst through the door and out into the cold night air. The glow of fire from lit up the sky, and my stomach dropped. "Doran, the cottage!"

"It doesn't matter," he said, shoving the middle of my back. "Keep going."

But as soon as we started running, several hulking black shapes emerged from the shadows, towering above us and blocking out the moon. The ground beneath our feet trembled as three giant shadowkin lumbered into the clearing. Their jaws dripped with fire, illuminating their giant, curved teeth. I raised my hands, but the enormous dogs did not flinch. Unlike the kerak, they would not burn easily.

Doran braced his feet on the ground. His head dropped, and his shoulders bunched as he curled his arms. Everything began to tremble, and I nearly lost my balance as wide cracks formed in the earth. The shadowkin stopped in their tracks, ears perked, and they began baying over the loud rumble. My fire died out, and Raisa clutched my shoulder tight, nearly dropping her torch. "Ailynn?"

"Go," I shouted, shoving her toward the tree line.

She let go of my arm and started running into the darkness. I followed close behind her, unwilling to let her out of my sight, but I cast a worried glance over my shoulder. Doran was still standing there, and his old body looked strong as an oak instead of old and frail. The shadowkin tried to lunge at him, but a loud rumble echoed through the trees, and the earth beneath them opened into a wide pit. They scrabbled at the sides of the hole, trying to haul their massive bulk over the edge, but they could not escape.

Doran turned to follow us, and I slowed my pace to wait for him. "How did you do that? I panted when he reached us. I had seen him lob chunks of stone and earth at me before, but I had not guessed the extent of his power.

"A lesson for another day, *Acha*. Where is Raisa?"

"Here," she said, clutching the pack tight to her chest. Her torch sputtered, threatening to die out. "Are there any more kerak? Or whatever those things were?"

"Shadowkin," I said. "We were lucky to escape. They don't burn easily."

"Did Mogra make them, too?" she whispered.

I nodded. Hearing Mogra's name reminded me of the glowing eyes of the kerak scout. There was no way to know for certain, I felt sure she had seen me through them. "I think most of the kerak were trapped in the cottage," I said, refusing to meet Doran's eyes. "I'm sorry about that. You know, she always told me I was bad at controlling my fire."

"Bad?" Doran snorted. "You're alive, aren't you?"

"We're all alive," Raisa said. "You were the one who got us out."

"Maybe, but what now? Where should we go?"

"Where I was going to take you in the first place." Doran began walking through the forest, heading toward a thinning tree line in the distance. I could barely make it out, even with the glow of the blazing cottage behind us. "This wood only stretches a few miles. After that, we'll head for Catyr Bane. It's the quickest way to Ardu."

"Ardu?" Raisa said, excitement clear in her voice. "But that means—"

"Yes," Doran said. "We're going to see the Liarre."

CHAPTER THREE

WE LEFT THE WOOD soon after the first rays of light peeked over the soft, blurred edges of the hilltops. I kept glancing over my shoulder, but we did not run into any more kerak. My mind kept flashing back to the claws hovering over Raisa's throat, and the steady hum of magic throbbed through my hands even though I did not need to summon my fire.

Raisa, however, seemed relatively cheerful. The exercise suited her, and I noticed a subtle darkening of her complexion after only a few hours in the morning sun. At first I thought to chastise her for her good mood, but then I realized this was the first proper walk she had taken in years. Despite everything, she was probably thankful to be free of her prison.

I could not bring myself to return her smiles. With Mogra and her beasts looking for us, I felt confined even outdoors. The gradual shifting of the landscape as the day wore on did not help. The hills became steeper, and the dirt beneath our feet was slowly replaced by reddish-brown rock. The horizon also changed. I could see the clear silhouette of mountains in the distance, although I had to lift my hand to shield my eyes from the blinding sun. They were not the familiar shape of the Rengast, but the jagged edges of Catyr Bane, the set of canyons and cliffs between western Amendyr and Liarre territory.

"When do we leave Amendyr?" I asked.

"Not for a while, but the city of Ardu is on the border. The Liarre Council is meeting there."

"The Liarre Council?" I asked, thinking back to something Cate had told me during my brief stay in the rebel camp. "That's why we're going there, isn't it?"

"Of course. Cate and Larna should be heading there themselves to attend the vote. Chairwoman Maresth has called all of the councilmembers together so that they can come to a decision."

Raisa looked at me, so I explained. "Cate and Larna are going to try and convince the Liarre to help the rebellion."

"Of course they will help the rebellion," she said, sounding more confident than I felt. "The Liarre are sensible creatures. If the Queen has all of Amendyr under her thumb, what's to stop her from crossing their border next?"

I shrugged. "Some Liarre aren't fond of humans. They might not want to waste their resources fighting a war in a foreign kingdom."

"No use worrying about it now," Doran said. "We're at least two weeks away from Ardu, and once they begin a debate, the Liarre can talk for at least another three."

"Two weeks?" I said. No map buried in the dusty pages of a book had prepared me for the reality of traveling across such a large area. At least during my journeys through the middle of the kingdom, I had been able to stop and rest in the little towns along the way. We would find no shelter in Catyr Bane. "We can't walk for two straight weeks. I might be able to manage, but Raisa—"

"Will be fine," she interrupted. "I'll walk as far as I need to."

I turned back to Doran. "Couldn't we fly? You controlled Mogra's great wind to bring us here. Surely you could summon one of your own."

Doran kept walking. "Such a force of magic would be like a beacon to Mogra's forces. They would find us in a matter of hours. Traveling without magic is the safest way." I began to protest, but Doran glanced at Raisa meaningfully when she was not looking, and then caught my eye. Suddenly, walking did not seem to be such a bad idea.

"At least the country will be less open once we reach Catyr Bane," I muttered, trying to find something good in the situation.

"True, but we'll have to remain on our guard. Wyverns live in the canyons there." The reminder ruined any of my positive thoughts. Wyverns were the smaller, less-intelligent cousins of the extinct dragons, and although only capable of the most rudimentary human speech, they were cunning and dangerous. They also ate human flesh when they could find it. "Yet another reason not to use a great wind."

"I don't mind," Raisa said, trying to reassure me. "Everything will be fine."

"Yes," I repeated, although I couldn't bring myself to sound enthusiastic. "Everything will be fine."

* * *

The days smeared together into a fog as we made our way west into the canyons. The cliffs and ridges of Catyr Bane were completely alien to me. Their jagged edges shielded us from the worst of the sun's glare, casting dark shadows even at midday, but the gorge's rocky outcroppings made perfect hiding places. I kept expecting a kerak or a wyvern to lunge out at us as we passed.

The new surroundings made me feel uneasy, but they delighted Raisa. She always took the time to point out interesting colors that swirled in the sheets of rock sprouting from the ground, memorizing landmarks and their proportions in order to draw them later. Although I remained tired and fearful, I did enjoy seeing her happy. While the landscape changed, Raisa's body also changed. Her pregnancy became more obvious with each passing day. I had seen and treated women with child before, but the swift, dramatic transformation of her figure astonished me.

Doran remained quiet and introspective, and since he chose not to dampen Raisa's optimistic attitude, I followed his silent example. At first, I thought she did not truly understand the danger we were in, but she soon corrected my mistake. As the sun started to set, she imitated my nervous behavior, plucking at the blue scarf around her neck and glancing to either side.

"What are you doing?" I asked, sitting down beside her as she rolled out her thin sleeping pallet. I caught a glimpse of something in her hand, and it took me a moment to make out the black bristles of the comb in the steadily creeping darkness. "Do you need me to take care of your hair for you?"

She shook her head, running her thumb back and forth over the comb's edge. "No. You and Doran have magic to protect you." Although her voice remained steady and calm, I could tell she was afraid. "What do I have? I'm no *Ariada*, and I don't know how to use any weapons. A comb isn't much, but it's better than nothing. If the kerak or something worse manage to find us here, I refuse to let them take me. I'll use whatever I can."

As I gazed into Raisa's tired face, I was struck by how much she had changed. She understood the perilous situation we were in, and I could not help admiring the unwavering optimism she displayed in spite of it. "You seemed to be doing well for yourself back at Doran's cottage," I reminded her. The memory still twisted inside my gut, but I put aside my own feelings of fear.

The corners of her lips twitched into a smile. "Well, I wasn't going to just stand there and die, I have too much to live for now."

"What do you mean?"

Raisa considered her answer, but she reached out for my hand through the silence. I allowed her to take it. "I have not been totally honest with you," she said at last. "I need to tell you why I...why I associated with Byron."

I flinched. Even now, the name stung like a slap. "Don't tell me you loved him," I said, averting my eyes.

"Don't be ridiculous, Ailynn. Of course I don't love him. I never did."

"He was using you," I said angrily. "He practically forced himself on you." This was not something I had considered, and I immediately felt regret for not bringing it up before. "Raisa, did he—"

"No, he didn't rape me. I never thought you were dead, Ailynn. I went months without hearing anything from you, but I couldn't bring myself to believe Mogra was telling the truth. That is the reason I entered into an arrangement with him. I wanted to find a way to escape so I could go look for you. He wasn't just using me. I was using him, too."

The color drained from my face. I had no idea whether this confession made things better or worse. It hurt to think that Raisa had shared a bed with Byron even while believing I was alive, but she had not lost faith in me. "Why didn't you tell me this?"

Raisa sighed. "Because I knew you would feel responsible. You have always taken responsibility for everything that has ever happened to me. I didn't want my attempts to escape and find you to weigh on you as well. It was my choice."

Despite what she was saying, the bitter taste of guilt burned the back of my throat. "If I hadn't left—"

Raisa tightened her grip. "You did what you needed to do in order to save me, just like I did what I needed to do in order to save myself. I know it must have hurt to find out about Byron, but I had no way of knowing where you were or if you were safe. If you were in danger, I wanted to be there to help. I just had to find a way to break the spell and find you. The woman who used to bring me food from the village told Byron about the beautiful maiden hidden in the forest, and when he came to see for himself..."

"If he killed Mogra, you would be free and you could look for me." I gave her a weak smile. "You read too many fairy stories."

"Well, the prince or nobleman's son always kills the evil witch." She bit down on her lower lip, and when she lifted her eyes to look at me, they were glistening. "Tell me you forgive me, Ailynn," she whispered. "I know I'm being selfish, but I need to hear it."

My emotions hung somewhere between pain, guilt, and relief with the knowledge that Raisa had not forgotten about me when I left. She had not taken Byron as a replacement because she thought I was never coming back. She had been trying to escape and come to me. As unlikely as it seemed, this conversation had begun to repair the damage between us. "I forgive you," I told her. "And I hope you'll forgive me, too."

"For what?"

"For making you feel terrible about what you did. I'm sure Byron's company was punishment enough."

Raisa laughed and squeezed my hand tighter, drawing it over into her lap. "You would be right about that. If there's a more pompous, arrogant man in all of Amendyr, I have yet to hear of him. And I hope you won't mind my telling you that you're a far better lover than he ever was."

The stab of hurt I had been expecting never came. Instead, I smiled. "Why would I mind a compliment? Although perhaps it's not fair to compare. I might be inexperienced, but an idiot like him was doomed from the start."

"I am glad you see it that way, Ailynn." She gestured at her stomach. "I know this has been hard for you. Not everyone would take back their lover while she was carrying someone else's child."

My voice became a low purr I had no idea I was capable of producing. "We aren't just lovers, *Tuathe*. And to be honest, you don't look entirely unappealing this way." I was a little embarrassed about that fact. Raisa's pregnancy was becoming more obvious with each passing day, but despite the rapid change, I still found her just as beautiful as I always had.

Raisa laughed. "I don't look entirely unappealing? Are you trying to tell me I'm beautiful, Ailynn?"

"Perhaps, but I think I did a poor job of it." Slowly, my touch trailed to the soft skin of her inner wrist. A flush rose in her cheeks, but her eyes darted off to the side, and I suddenly remembered that Doran was only a short distance away, setting up his own pallet. Although he had his back turned to us and stood too far away to hear our whispered words, the reminder of his presence distracted me from my train of thought. "I wish we were alone," I sighed, moving Raisa's hair to place a kiss behind her ear. The brush of my lips against her skin made her shiver. "But maybe it's a good thing that we need to wait. The first times were a little rushed."

"You want to touch me just because you care for me, not because you want to reassure yourself that I still belong to you. I understand."

"Am I crazy?"

Raisa's blush deepened. "Maybe, but I don't mind. How about I hold you while we fall asleep together instead? You could even tell me a story."

I grinned, reminded of a hundred other times when she had posed the same question while we were growing up. "Aren't you a little old for bedtime stories?"

"You can never be too old for bedtime stories," she insisted.

I eased down onto the sleeping pallet, and she curled against my side, staring up into the nighttime sky. This time, there were no shadows to hide the stars, and their light shone across our faces. "If that's true, why don't you tell me one instead?"

"All right, then. Which one do you want to hear?"

My eyes began sorting through the constellations until I found the one I was looking for. I raised my hand and pointed. "I want to hear the story of Reagan and Saweya."

"Ailynn, are you sure?" Raisa asked. I could hear a hint of nervousness in her voice. She knew my memories of that particular story were entwined with memories of Byron.

I nodded. "Yes. That's the one I want to hear."

"All right." Raisa took a deep breath and began the tale. "Reagan's tongue flicked next to the frightened youth's cheek, her gleaming teeth reflecting the bright noon sun. Her scales shifted, not even scratched by the boy's blade, enchanted though it was. His weapon had long-since been discarded, and he lay defenseless and trembling at the mighty dragon's feet. Never one to kill needlessly, Reagan lifted her proud head and roared, sending great showers of rock tumbling down the sides of the nearest mountains. 'Run,' she said to the boy, 'run or I will feast upon your pathetic carcass and leave your bones to bleach in the sun...'"

CHAPTER FOUR

THE SUN SANK BELOW the horizon as afternoon crept into evening. The shadows lengthened from beneath the base of the cliffs, leaving black streaks over the ground. It had been two weeks since we had left Doran's house, and being in a constant state of alertness exhausted me. Journeying on foot drained more of our energy with each day, and Raisa and Doran were both beginning to show signs of weariness as our supplies dwindled.

"We should find somewhere to stop and rest," I said, looking forward to a mouthful of food and a few hours of sleep. "I'm not sure how much further we can go."

Doran looked as though he was about to disagree, but Raisa spoke up. "You and Ailynn could have another training session," she said. "At least we wouldn't be wasting the rest of the daylight."

I groaned at the thought. Doran had continued my 'education'— that is, throwing things at me and sending me crashing into the cliff side—during our journey, and although I improved each time, I still ended up aching by the time we finished. "Not today," I muttered. "I need to rest before my body takes any more punishment." My legs protested with every step, and if I felt this way, I could not even imagine how tired Raisa and Doran must be.

Doran scanned the narrow passageway between the cliffs. It had grown thinner and thinner throughout the day, and there was barely enough room for us to walk beside each other. Many of the crags and crevices dotting the sides of the canyon before had dissolved into smooth red rock, leaving only the footpath. "I don't see any cover." He sighed. "We shouldn't stop here. It's too exposed."

A loud scraping sound came from somewhere above us. My heart began pounding, and my head whipped up as I tried to spot the source of the noise. Raisa drew closer to my side, removing the comb she kept at her belt. "What was that? A kerak?"

"I don't think so."

A large black shadow swooped overhead, expanding around our feet. "Kee-lum!"

Hot, tearing pain ripped across my back, hooking in to my shirt and scoring my flesh. I screamed, and somewhere behind me, Doran shouted a Word of Power. The biting scent of magic filled the air, and the thing on top of me fell to one side. I dragged myself to my feet, staring down at an enormous, scaly mass. It writhed and thrashed over the ground like a giant snake, but amidst the dust, I could make out two sharp talons and a pair of leathery wings. We had seen flocks of wyvern high overhead during the last few days, but none had come close enough to attack us.

My first instinct was to place myself in front of Raisa. She did not argue, taking several steps backward until she was pressed against the vertical wall of the canyon, watching the wyvern with wide eyes. "Kee-lum!" it clicked again, its side fins puffing out from its leathery neck.

I began to summon my fire, but hesitated when I saw the plumes of smoke trailing from the creature's nose. I doubted fire would do much to hurt it. To my surprise, the first memory that flashed into my mind was of the great wind that Mogra had used to lift Raisa and me into the sky. I jerked the threads of magic surrounding us and pushed a wave of air toward the creature.

The wyvern weighed almost nothing, and the sharp gust shoved it back several feet. Its claws scrabbled against the canyon wall, and it lifted its snout, letting out a series of sharp whistles and clacks. Suddenly, three more wyvern dove down from the sky and landed on the cliff's face. I braced myself beside Doran and held my ground, waiting for them to charge. To my surprise, they clicked and hissed their displeasure. "Keelum! Kriii!" They circled around us, tails lashing, obviously trying to decide what to do.

The wyvern I had blown back managed to find its balance and hobble about, waving its wings at us and clacking its beak. The rest of the flock decided to join it, launching off the cliff's face and landing on the ground beside their wounded companion. All four of them stretched out their wings and fins, sucking air into their chests and trying to look as large as possible. They jabbered and clicked at each other with wild sounds that almost seemed like a language.

"Stay still," Doran whispered, edging slowly toward me. "They're sky hunters, and they see through movement." The light around us was fading and I felt a small lift of hope. If we waited them out, perhaps they would leave once they could no longer see us.

Just when I thought we might be safe, the wyvern charged. Doran and I tried to push the beasts away from us with short gusts of air, but it proved useless. They were light and easy to hit, but they recovered their balance quickly. After a minute, we had made no progress, and I sported a shallow cut on my arm. The wyvern darted back and forth, not interested in a quick killing blow. They wanted to tire us out, and I began to worry that their strategy might work.

As the last of the sunlight disappeared, a loud shout echoed through the canyon pathway. The wyvern lifted their heads, but before they could move, a flight of arrows arched through the air above them. Most of the shafts hit their mark, and the wyvern squealed with pain, thrashing blindly as they tried to escape. One managed to lift off the ground, but the other three collapsed to the canyon floor. The bodies twitched, then went still.

Raisa stared at the fallen wyvern. "Who did that?"

Doran smiled. "Look."

I obeyed, and my eyes widened when I saw exactly who had saved us. A band of warriors approached at a run from the other end of the canyon, and the creature at their head was something out of legend. An equiarre, half man and half horse, tall, proud, and infinitely more wild and beautiful than any depiction I had seen in a book or on a tapestry. His bare chest flashed in the moonlight, his lower body a dappled gray. His face seemed human, but the angles were wrong. His features seemed stretched out, not ugly, but noticeably different. He held a beautiful bow in his left hand, and a quiver of arrows was lashed to his back.

"Well met, Doran," the equiarre said. "It looks like Rachari was right and we found you just in time."

Doran stepped forward, clasping hands with the large creature. "Well met, Hassa. I was wondering when you, Jinale, and the others would show up."

Once I got over my shock, I stared at the other creatures standing around the equiarre. They were all a strange mixture of human and animal. One was vaguely reptilian, with fangs, scales, and a long, winding tail. A forked tongue flicked from between his thin lips. Another had the long, sleek form of a cat, and its paws looked almost as large as my head. Yet another had the black, bulbous body of an enormous spider. She supported herself on eight legs, and the eye tattoos on her cheeks stood out even in the dim light.

"Thank you for saving us," I said, trying to hide my nervousness.

The spider opened her mouth to speak, and I shivered as I noticed the pair of needle-like fangs curling over her lower lip. "You are welcome, humani. You looked like you were having some trouble. I'm not surprised. The wyvern have come here in greater numbers since the sightings started."

"The sightings?" I asked. "What sightings?"

"Sightings of the witch," Hassa explained. "She prowls the shadows here, waiting. Now, we know what she was waiting for." The large equiarre gave me a thorough but unthreatening examination. "Hello, young witch," he said, offering his large hand for me to clasp. I did so weakly, still trying to sustain my balance. He noticed, and did not grip very hard, although I could sense the strength in his thick fingers. "I believe I have met some friends of yours."

"Cate and Larna?"

He nodded. "They arrived safely at Ardu four days ago."

"Four days?" I asked, surprised by how quickly they had traveled.

"Wyr travel faster than humani," the great spider said. "We did not have an opportunity to meet with them for long. The one with the glowing red mane asked us to come here. Apparently, her instincts were right."

My body shuddered and Raisa moved her steadying hand from my arm to my back. When it came away red with blood, she gasped. "Ailynn, you're still bleeding."

The edges of my vision were growing fuzzy, and I allowed her to help me sit down near the edge of the canyon. "Dry dressing for the wound," I said, leaning my head back against the vertical sheet of rock. "If there's infection, then we can see about a poultice."

For all of my experience with treating wounds, including my own burns, I was a very poor patient. I allowed Raisa to clean the wound on my back, but it hurt, and I complained and fussed under her gentle hands. It bled freely, and after she had bandaged it, we removed my ruined shirt. While I instructed Raisa, the Liarre began to build a makeshift camp. They rolled out the sleeping pallets, dug small pits, and carried their supplies closer to us.

"Ailynn?" Raisa asked as she helped me pull a new shirt over my head. Discreetly, so that no one would see, she nodded at the huge, spider-like woman. Her large, hairy bulk was surprisingly quick and coordinated as she moved through the camp and I suspected she would be able to scale the canyon walls. "Tell me, is she looking at me?"

"I think it's just the eye tattoos," I mumbled under my breath.

Raisa sighed. "I know she isn't dangerous, but I suppose I didn't expect her to be so large. When I think of Liarre, I picture equiarre or feliarre, not giant spiders," she whispered.

"I suppose arachniarre are too frightening for children's stories," I said, wincing as I shifted my shoulder. No heat surrounded the wound, and I hoped it would not become infected.

"Frightening is right," said the arachniarre. She approached us on eight thick, hairy legs with a bend in the middle. Raisa's eyes grew large, but to her credit, she did not look fearful otherwise. "There are many stories about us, little humani, but your mate is right. We make your kind uncomfortable." She grinned, revealing a glimpse of her black tongue.

Raisa's surprise changed to embarrassment at being overheard. "I find you rather impressive, actually."

"Really?" The arachniarre's large mouth curled around the words in a curious accent, one that I had never heard before. "My name is Jinale. Hassa and I were sent here to find you. The shaman and her *Tuathe* will be glad to hear that we were successful."

"We were on our way to see them," I said.

Jinale's intimidating smile remained. "Yes, but now you will travel faster."

"You would allow us to ride you?" Raisa asked, clearly surprised by the offer. Jinale nodded. "That is an honor and a privilege. We would be incredibly grateful."

"As you should be," said the spider, but her facial expression— what I could read of the strange planes and angles, anyway—seemed friendly and not menacing. "We will carry you and the young mother-to-be. For now, we will set up camp."

Rae D. Magdon

CHAPTER FIVE

"WHAT ARE YOU DOING, Raisa?

Raisa continued staring at Hassa with a curious expression as he stood beyond the fire pit, discussing something with Doran. The firelight moved over her face, bringing the points of her cheeks forward and casting the sides into shadow as she turned to look at me. "I'm studying his proportions. "The Liarre are fascinating creatures. I want to remember what they look like so that I can draw them."

I smiled, remembering some of the other drawings that Raisa had shared with me. The ones of us in intimate positions were my favorites, but all of her artwork was beautiful. "Are you sad about losing your work?"

"Yes, but I would trade them all for the real thing." Her eyes wandered back to Doran, and I saw a hint of sadness creep into her eyes. "I think Doran is going to leave us now that we are with the Liarre."

"How do you know?" I had sensed the same thing. Even now, he was gesturing back and forth from us to the rest of the camp as he talked with Hassa.

Raisa shrugged. "He's an old man. I know he's powerful, but I've seen how tired travelling has made him. He shouldn't be here."

"You're right. He should be at home, or what's left of his home, anyway," I said, a pang of guilt wrenching my stomach.

"I'm sure he's resourceful enough to rebuild it," Raisa said. "To be honest, I wondered if you would ask me to go back with him."

My chest tightened. "What do you mean? Why would I want you to go back?"

"I'm the one Mogra wants."

"She will probably seek me out anyway. I escaped with her greatest treasure. She cannot let me remain alive. It would be a wound to her pride if nothing else. Don't you want to stay with me?"

Raisa rolled her eyes. "Don't be stupid, Ailynn, of course I want to stay with you. Sometimes, though, I can't help but wonder if your life would be better without me."

The confession pierced my heart. I took her hand in mine and gripped it tight. "Never. My life would never be better for having lost you." My words failed me, and I glanced toward one of the tents the Liarre had assembled. For what I wanted to say, we would need more privacy. "Come with me," I murmured, helping Raisa to her feet. She kept hold of my arm even once she had found her balance, and the warmth of her hand made my skin burn beneath the fabric of my shirt.

Once we were alone inside of the tent, Raisa let go of me. "Well? What did you want to say?"

I wanted to tell Raisa what I couldn't bring myself to say in the cave. I wanted to confess that I loved her. To reassure her that our rocky start did not matter. To promise I would help raise the child she was carrying, and vow to stay with her for the rest of our lives. But when I opened my mouth, the words refused to come. They stuck in my chest, and I let out a half-broken sound instead.

Raisa wrapped me in her arms, resting her head against my shoulder as she held me tight. "Oh, Ailynn...I'm so sorry—"

"No." My voice cracked with the effort of speaking around the tight lump in my throat. "No. You don't need to be sorry anymore. I just..." The pressure inside my chest built until I could feel each throb of my heartbeat, and my lips trembled, torn between smiling and sobbing. "I...I love you." I had said the words once before back in the cave, but they meant something different this time. They were more than just an expression of my feelings. They were an offer of forgiveness, a promise I had not been brave enough to make until now.

Raisa looked up at me in confusion. "I love you, too, Ailynn."

"You don't understand," Suddenly, all the words that I had been holding back came pouring from my mouth. "I *love* you. I want to be with you. I want to raise the baby with you. And I never want to leave your side again."

Raisa's eyes widened in shock, and she took a nervous step back, letting her hands slide down to clutch the sides of my arms. "Don't make promises you can't keep," she whispered. Her voice shook with fear, but her eyes shimmered with hope. "I told you once before, I don't think I'll survive if I lose you again."

"You won't lose me," I promised. "I want to say with you, and the baby, forever. I'm yours, *Tuathe*. I've always been yours."

Tears poured down Raisa's cheeks, but a smile stretched across her cheeks. She leaned forward and buried her face in my shirt, and I took her in my arms. "I love you," she mumbled into my chest. The fabric muffled the words, but hearing them made my heart sing.

I rocked her in my embrace until her crying stopped and her breathing returned to normal. I had to swipe at my own eyes with my sleeve, and she laughed when she caught me brushing my tears away. "We've ruined your shirt between the two of us," she teased, her voice still a little hoarse. "Maybe I should help you take it off?"

I stepped back, linking my hands with hers for just a moment to extend our contact before I let go and pulled the shirt over my head. This time, there was no self-consciousness. I had already bared my heart to Raisa, baring my body was no different. I let it fall to the floor, taking pride in the expression of wonder that crossed her face. I knew Raisa saw me the same way I had always seen her, as someone beautiful.

After a long moment, she shook herself out of staring and began removing her own clothes, although her eyes never left me. I made quick work of my leggings, nearly tripping over them in my haste. At last, we came together, skin meeting skin. I could feel the force of her love just as strongly as the warmth of her body against mine. For the first time, I felt no barriers between us.

My legs trembled, and Raisa eased us down onto the floor of the tent. I nearly collapsed on top of her, but I managed to catch my weight on my arms at the last moment. "Sorry," I said, offering her an embarrassed smile. She kissed me. I did not need to speak anymore. I had finally said everything I needed to say.

I stroked my hands along her sides, drinking in the soft heat of her skin through my palms. Her arms curled around my neck, tangling through my hair to keep my lips against hers. She needn't have bothered. I couldn't stop kissing her, not even when my lungs burned for air. One of her calves curled around mine, and her knee lifted to press between my legs. A low throbbing began inside me, a deep ache in my core. The contact made me groan, and she rubbed circles over my back until I grew accustomed to it.

Her hands slid lower, cupping the swell of my backside and urging me to move. The first push of my hips finally made me break our kiss and gasp for breath. A surge of heat spilled out of me, slickening Raisa's thigh. I knew she felt it, because the edges of her nails dug tighter into my flesh and her body trembled beneath mine. The next stroke was more like gliding, and with her help, I fell into a slow rhythm. Before I lost myself in her, I slid one of my hands between our bodies, pausing to caress the swell of her stomach as my fingertips wandered lower. "I want to show you," I whispered. "I want to show you how much I love you."

She gazed up at me with such love in her eyes that my movements almost faltered. "Ailynn, you already have."

My fingers slipped between her legs, and I gasped at the well of heat I found within her. She hooked a knee around my waist, opening herself to me as her legs tangled with mine. She brought one of her own hands down to replace her thigh, and I slid forward at the same moment she did. The dual sensations, filling and being filled, were almost too difficult to separate. I did not want to separate them. I wanted us to share everything, to feel everything.

I struggled to please her at first, focusing intently on the movement of my hand and ignoring hers, but after a while, I simply surrendered to instinct. When she began curling forward, finding the sensitive spot along my front wall, I did the same, shifting the angle of my wrist so I could swipe my thumb over her swollen tip. A shiver echoed between us, rolling from her body into mine. She clutched down around my fingers, drawing tighter with every thrust, and I did the same, rocking my hips forward to take her as deep inside of me as I could. Our bodies knew each other, and we moved as one.

All of a sudden, I couldn't breathe, and the pounding between my legs drowned out everything else. I had just enough control left to give Raisa one last push. She cried out and arched beneath me, freezing as pleasure carried her away. A flood poured out around my fingers, and I came a moment later, pulsing into her palm.

But it was not enough. Not nearly enough. Both of us kept moving without stopping to draw breath. We remained locked together, clutching each other desperately as we rode through our shared peak. Fresh tears spilled from my eyes, and although my vision was blurry, I could just make out the soft red curve of her lips as she smiled up at me. This closeness was what I had been longing for. This love was what I had needed all along.

At last, our waves faded to aftershocks, and we collapsed into a tangled heap. I rolled to the side, afraid I would put too much pressure on her stomach, but Raisa refused to let me go, folding me in her arms until I sighed and relaxed on top of her. I dipped down to rest my forehead against hers, and her laughter tickled my cheek.

"What are you laughing about?" I carefully removed my hand from between her legs. She made a noise of protest and closed her thighs around my wrist, preventing me from leaving.

"Nothing. I just can't remember the last time I was so happy. You really meant what you said earlier, didn't you? About staying with me, with us, forever?"

"Yes, I really meant it." And it was the truth. Instead of being terrified of what our future might hold, hope and joy filled me instead. As long as our life together had moments like this, I wanted it.

CHAPTER SIX

A SOFT NUDGE TO my shoulder jolted me out of a deep slumber. Doran's wrinkled face peered down at me, a colorless silhouette against the fuzzy gray skyline.

"You're leaving," I said.

He nodded. "You don't need me anymore, Ailynn. I'm headed back to my cottage, or what's left of it, at any rate." My face must have shown concern, because he explained further. "I will call the wind to carry me this time. You don't have to worry about me travelling alone through the canyons, *Acha*."

The word sent a pang of regret through my chest. "I will miss you." I sat up and rubbed my eyes to see him more clearly in the early morning darkness. I found myself trying to memorize his face. "Do you really have to go? I'm sure you would be welcome in Ardu with us."

He shook his head. "My place is not in Ardu. Hassa and the others will make sure you get there safely, and Cate and Larna will take good care of you there. Does Raisa still have the combs and the scarf I gave her?"

I glanced over at Raisa. The blue scarf was still around her neck, and I had used both of the combs to keep her long hair in some semblance of order. "Yes, she still has them."

"Good. Tell her to keep them close. They can only give their magic once. After that, you will have to use what I have taught you to protect her."

"All right," I said, trying to sound more confident than I felt. Although I had improved over the past few weeks, my abilities still seemed limited.

"Magic always comes when we call on it for protection," Doran said, reading my doubts. "You can do great things to save the ones you love."

"Will I see you again?"

He nodded. "I think so. Farewell, *Acha.*"

He gave me his blessing, touching both of my cheeks and kissing my forehead and I felt the keen edge of loss. For some reason, this man had touched me in ways I could not understand. Maybe it was because he had loved my mother long ago. He had been another witness to her tragic descent into madness.

Doran left without any great fanfare or a violent burst of magic. He simply walked east, the outline of his figure becoming smaller and smaller as it approached the brightening horizon line, which was beginning to brim over with sunlight. It was all very surreal, and I wondered if I was caught somewhere between dreams until Raisa stirred.

"He's gone, isn't he?" Raisa murmured, rubbing a soft patch of skin above of my leggings. I nodded, realized her eyes were still closed, and voiced my thoughts instead.

"You were right."

"I am sure he will be fine."

I sighed, but concern still washed over me. Mogra's threat loomed over all of us, and by protecting us from her, the old wizard had made himself a target. "Would you like to know a secret?"

Raisa opened her eyes. They were beautiful, and for a moment, I was overwhelmed with the sudden desire to kiss her. Then Raisa blinked. "What is it?"

"I wished that he was my father. Doran told me that he loved my mother once, before, you know, before she became what she is."

"Did you ask him?"

"No. I was hoping he would tell me. Or maybe I was just afraid he would say no." I had no idea whether Doran was my father or not. He did not look like me, and I might have inherited all of my magical aptitude from my mother. Even so, I could not help wondering. I looked so much like Mogra I had never really wondered who my father was before. I could not remember asking her, and isolated in the Forest, I had never felt his absence in my life. Now, I regretted that emptiness.

"Do you ever wish to find out about your parents?" I asked, almost afraid of the answer.

"Sometimes I wonder about them." I remembered back to when

Raisa had first asked about her parents, all those years ago. Mogra had lied to her. It was entirely possible that, if I had asked the same question about my father, she would have lied to me as well. Perhaps I had known this deep inside, even as a growing child, and that was why I had never bothered. "But you were enough for me. You were my everything, even if we weren't related by blood."

I smiled weakly. "I understand. Back then, you were simply mine." The word twisted my lips, and I averted my eyes. It sounded like something Mogra would say. I could only hope my feelings for Raisa were different than her delusions of ownership.

"What's wrong, Ailynn?" Raisa asked, stroking the side of my arm.

I let out a long sigh. "Nothing, love. Nothing at all."

Raisa was silent for a long moment, and then a mischievous smile lit up her face. "If Doran was your father, do you know what that means?"

"No, what?"

"It means your father caught you naked in bed with me and threw clothes on top of your head."

I groaned, trying not to disturb the rest of our little campsite. "Please, don't remind me," I muttered, but despite my embarrassment, her teasing had cheered me up. I gave her a soft nudge. "Come on, up with you. We'd better go and find something to eat before the rest of the camp is ready to start moving."

* * *

Fairy stories never describe the boring parts of going on an adventure. The heroes always seem to skip right to the exciting events. They do not have to worry about rationing food, and their feet are never sore from walking. They can travel from one place to another in the blink of an eye. But, of course, we were not in a fairy tale. Along with everything else came the mundane—traveling, packing and re-packing, sleeping on the ground in temperatures too hot or too cold.

One bright spot stood out amidst the monotony, however. Joining up with the party of Liarre warriors made our progress much faster since we were allowed to ride. This surprised me, because all of the literature I had read clearly stated the Liarre hated being viewed as beasts of burden, and having a human mount them was seen as demeaning.

Knowing this, I made sure to thank Hassa profusely when he

offered to carry me. Not only was he going against his people's customs, but he was also sparing my legs, and the least I could do was show my gratitude. The other Liarre accepted the decision to let us ride without too much protest, although I heard one or two of the caniarre, dog-men with wicked looking teeth and bulging muscles under sleek fur, complaining under their breath.

Raisa was also polite and, fortunately for me, had no objections to riding on Jinale. Although the arachniarre seemed very likable, the sight of her made me understand why the Liarre were so revered in Amendyrri legends. She looked like something out of a tapestry scene or a painting.

Raisa's fearlessness surprised me, particularly since her pregnancy was becoming more and more pronounced every day. I questioned her, but was unable to pin down the exact date of conception any closer than fourteen or fifteen weeks. She seemed unusually far along for that amount of time. When she mentioned she could feel the baby moving inside of her, the shock within me grew deeper.

"Already?" I silently asked for permission to touch her stomach, which she granted. The curve of her belly was stretching and hardening. Anyone looking at her could tell she was carrying a child now, even though the shirt she wore was loose around her hips

"Is something wrong?"

"No, nothing serious." I pressed my lips together. I thought I could feel the position of a head, and once or twice I imagined I could feel the soft bumps and taps of the baby's limbs moving underneath her muscles. "Are you sure you might not be farther along than you think? Fifteen weeks is early for me to feel quickening on the outside, especially since this is your first child."

Raisa shrugged. "Fifteen weeks ago is the closest I can place it. There were not that many opportunities that might have resulted in this." Despite her awkward wording, I was a little relieved. It still hurt to think of Raisa sharing her body with someone I despised, and it helped to know it had only happened a few times. Still, I wrinkled my nose and frowned. The baby kicked again. "Stop making that face. You are upsetting him."

"Him?" I asked. "How do you know it will be a him?"

"You call the baby a him all the time, Ailynn. I was just copying you."

"I like the idea of a boy." I did not need to add that my own relationship with my mother had turned out very badly, and I did not

162

have faith I would be a good example for a girl to follow.

As it turned out, Raisa's pregnancy turned out to be a point in our favor with the Liarre. Some of them had unfavorable opinions of humans, understandable considering some of the things our race had tried to do to their people over the years. However, it seemed even the most belligerent caniarre or fearsome arachniarre smiled when they saw my lover and the new life growing inside of her.

"From the look of you, humani babies are very tiny," Jinale commented as Raisa rode on her back. "Liarre children are much larger, even inside of their mothers."

"Do you have any children?" Raisa asked.

"No, but Hassa does."

"My mate and I have two daughters," Hassa said. I could feel his voice vibrate through the core of his body beneath where I was sitting. I wondered if I would ever be able to speak about Raisa's children with such pride in my voice. I already felt more affection for the unborn life than I had anticipated, but could I accept him as my own? I had no part in making him, but perhaps I could shape his young mind as he began to learn and grow.

"Do you worry that they take on your bad qualities as well as the good qualities you try to teach them?"

"Yes," he said after a moment's thought. "Foals learn by example. They copy what they see."

"What if the example they were set is a poor one?"

Hassa seemed to sense the serious nature of the question, because he continued to ponder it for several steps. "Then they must be their own example. Some will never know anything else, but the stronger ones are not doomed to repeat their parents' mistakes."

Glancing over my shoulder, I watched Raisa riding on Jinale. Raisa's golden hair fell well past her waist, draping over the spider's side. I already knew she would be a good and loving example for the baby growing inside of her. She was smart, resourceful, and endlessly creative. Any child of hers would surely become someone good. Hopefully, I could follow her example.

Suddenly, a few of the Liarre beside us stiffened. A feliarre nearby crouched down, hackles rising, ears pricked up to listen. I stiffened too, but for a different reason. A dark shadow hung over our heads. As one, the party looked up. Tiny black dots circled above us, watching and waiting.

"Are those more wyvern?" I asked. "I thought we'd seen the last of them."

Hassa did not respond, but he reached for the bow strapped across his back. Jinale did the same, reaching to pull an arrow from the quiver she carried with her. "Get off of my back," she told Raisa. "Climb up with Ailynn. Hassa is faster than the rest of us." She left the rest of the message unspoken, but it was clear enough. If the Wyvern decided to attack us, she wanted us to run.

Raisa obeyed the order. I offered her my hand and helped her up in front of me. Hassa did not react to the extra weight, but watched the open landscape, moving his head from side to side.

"Look behind you," Hassa shouted.

Both of us turned. A giant black cloud rolled toward us from between the walls of the canyons we had left behind, crawling over the flat northern plains. A low, ominous rumbling came with it, echoing like thunder. It moved impossibly fast, covering the ground at an alarming speed.

"It has to be enchanted," I said.

Creatures emerged from the darkness, kerak and enormous shadowkin, close enough for us to see their crouched forms against the black, smoky body of the cloud. The Liarre all drew their bows, even Hassa, and Raisa had to lean back into me to avoid his elbow as his arm reached back. He drew an arrow from his quiver, drawing it to the point and releasing it into the rapidly darkening air. A feral howl followed moments later, but I could not see where the arrow had hit its mark. The cloud continued stretching up to the sky, growing larger by the second and blocking out the sunlight. The strong, violent trembling of magic became stronger, and its bitter smell curled in my nose.

"Mogra is coming," I told Hassa. "I can feel her."

"Hold steady," he said, letting another arrow fly. "We haven't seen her yet."

To my surprise, the large shadowkin began to fall. One of them toppled over as soon as one of Jinale's arrows grazed its flesh, and I didn't understand until I noticed her sucking on the tip of her next arrow. So, her fangs were filled with poison. Although the arrows wounded the kerak, it did not stop them. They continued forward in starts and jerks even with the shafts of the arrows sticking out of their bodies. Thirty yards, twenty...*Fire. They need fire.*

"Light your arrows," I shouted, feeling the familiar rush of power as I tugged on the threads of magic surrounding me, snapping them in a release of energy until my hands were surrounded in balls of flame.

Holding out both of my arms, I allowed Hassa to dip one of his arrows in the magical fire until it took hold. This time, when he let his arrow fly, it hit the closest kerak in the center of its chest. The creature howled as it burst into flame, disintegrating into a pile of ash.

Although Jinale continued using her poisoned arrows to take down the shadowkin, the other Liarre began using my fire as well. The first wave of kerak fell, and for a moment, there was nothing but the cloud and the tiny black dots circling overhead. Then another wave came. And another. They poured from the mouth of the cloud in an endless wave, too fast for the arrows to cut down.

"We are running out," Hassa said, lighting one of his final shafts. Soon, the Liarre would only be left with short-ranged weapons.

"If the witch comes out of that cloud, you need to run with the humani," Jinale said as she removed the tip of an arrow from her mouth, her last one as well. "It's your only chance."

"I promised Rachari I would protect you," Hassa protested.

Jinale's eyes narrowed to slits. "You told Cate you would bring her friends to Ardu safely. You are faster than any of us. We will try to buy you some time."

"But—" A loud, high-pitched wail interrupted him. A massive black shadowkin, larger than any of the others, exploded out of the dark, foul smoke. Its heavy paw steps made the ground tremble. On its back was a woman, unnaturally tall, wrapped in black robes and crowned by a ring of fire. I squinted to make out her face in the patches of light flashing around us. My memory filled in the details I could not see from a distance. Mogra was old and young at the same time, constantly shifting like a warped reflection in a pool.

"Run," Jinale shouted.

Hassa turned around and began running, carrying us over the plains and leaving the party behind.

CHAPTER EIGHT

I BENT LOW OVER Hassa's back, clinging to his waist. His hooves drummed over the uneven ground, his body heaving. The shadows of the wyverns hovered over us like monstrous birds, swallowing us up as we hurtled over the plains. Raisa pulled closer to me, her long golden hair whipping against my face, and I could hear her fearful breaths beside my ear. "Ailynn, behind us."

I looked back over my shoulder. A shadowkin was charging after us, fire dripping from its huge jaws. Mogra was perched on its neck, her black robes flying behind her like the tattered wings of a raven. Once again, she was a strange mix of old and young, ugly and beautiful. The distance between us closed with each passing heartbeat, and hatred twisted her face.

There was no time. Doran had warned us not to use his three gifts until the need was greatest, but if Mogra caught us, she would kill us. "Raisa, the comb." I felt Raisa shift behind me, and I turned my head just in time to see her pull the first comb from her pocket. She threw it as far as she could and I held my breath.

With a loud crack and a low, deep rumble, the ground began to shake beneath us. The circling Wyverns screeched, flying higher in the sky and momentarily abandoning the chase. The ground split open and huge, thorny trees sprung from deep beneath the earth, reaching up into the sky. Like the sharp spikes of the little black comb, they stretched out in an endless straight line, blocking Mogra's path.

The rumbling behind us ceased. Mogra's frustrated screams carried through the giant thorn trees and over the empty stretch of the plains. There was another wave of sharp, hot magic, and a huge gust of air almost knocked the three of us to the ground. Miraculously, Hassa managed to keep his balance. Raisa and I were almost thrown from his back, but somehow we managed to remain astride. I risked a second glance back over my shoulder. A fierce, howling wind blew apart the trees, creating a pathway through the thorns. Mogra urged the shadowkin forward again, and the beast cleared the rest aside with several swipes of its giant paws. We had slowed her, but not stopped her.

The equiarre were fast, built for running and speed, but I could tell that Hassa was beginning to tire. Carrying two fully-grown women on his back, one with child, had sapped his strength. "If you have...any more ideas...or magic..." he panted as Mogra began to regain the ground she had lost. "Use it now."

Raisa shoved her hand into her pocket and reached for the brown comb, letting it fly behind us. This time, the ground began to change, growing slick and moist beneath Hassa's hooves. He adjusted his gait to stay on top of the thick mud, but we began sinking as a large, sticky brown pool of swamp water pooled around us. It blossomed out like a puddle of rain, growing larger every second until it became a river of sludge. Hassa managed to clamber up onto the far bank just in time, sighing as we returned to solid ground.

"Is she crossing?" Raisa asked.

I hoped not, but my instincts told me that a swamp would not be enough to stop Mogra's pursuit. The shadowkin was clawing its way through the muck, baying as it fought to lift its giant paws. Fire flared above its head as Mogra burned through her rage, but she was not near enough to send the blaze toward us. Then, I realized her plan. She was drying out the swamp beneath the shadowkin's feet. After a few moments, the beast charged forward again, sprinting after us at a terrifying speed.

Raisa clutched at the only item we had left, the blue scarf around her neck. We were running out of options, and unless we came up with a way to halt her permanently, we were as good as dead. I wanted to tell Raisa I loved her, but I shook the thought away. Now was not the time, when we were fleeing for our lives.

"I love you," I told her anyway. I looked into her eyes, and for a single moment, the sounds around us faded away.

Raisa gave me the only words I needed to hear. "I love you, too." She unwound the blue scarf from around her shoulders. The wind almost tore it from her hand, but her fingers held on tight to the fabric, refusing to let go. When Mogra drew so close I could see the pits of her eyes, she let the scarf fly.

The earth began to shake again, pieces of rock jutting up from the ground and pushing us forward and down. Hassa lost his balance. We fell, pushed forward by an enormous avalanche of earth. The ground rippled and shuddered, yawning open into a wide, gaping pit. The three of us clung to each other, but the mass of stone and dirt continued falling.

"Secutem!" The Word of Power blazed along my tongue, and a shield of air curled around us, weaving together like a net. Fire rushed along its length, searing through the falling debris. It ate into my skin, burning in my muscles and searing my skin. The magical threads pulled tighter and tighter, threatening to snap as the fire consumed everything it touched. Then, silence echoed in my ears, the flames died out, and darkness swallowed everything around me.

* * *

One star shone down on me, its cold, pale light washing over my face in ghostly, gray-white sheets. I shivered, wrapping my arms around myself to keep warm. The dim velvet sky became a shimmering black lake, and I could see my features reflected in the endless pool. Suddenly, my eyes and my cheeks rippled, changing and reforming as another face. Mogra stared back at me, swallowing the faint light of the star in the black pits of her eyes.

I touched my cheek. So did she. My lips parted. So did hers.

"Ailynn, my daughter." I heard the hiss of her voice in the whispering wind.

"I want nothing to do with you," I tried to sound braver than I felt. I had no idea whether I was navigating through a dream or some other reality, but I was afraid.

"You are disgusted with me," Mogra said. Her face disappeared, and she materialized in front of me instead, forming a solid shape as she emerged from the darkness. "But the same darkness lives in you, Ailynn. We are not so different."

I turned my back on her, unwilling to look. Seeing my face merged with hers was too much to bear. "I am not you," I protested, but my voice grew weak. Whether this was real or imagined did not matter. It had cut to the bone of my deepest, most secret fears.

"Oh, but you are, blood of my blood, flesh of my flesh." Her voice

169

hissed in my ear, snakes' tongues in the wind. "You stole my treasured girl, my princess. She will corrupt you and poison your heart with jealousy."

"No!" I whirled around, but there was only a wide field grass rippling around my ankles. She had disappeared.

Was it true? Doubts began creeping into my mind. The ice became fire, racing through my veins and bleeding beneath my skin. My body ached as I remembered how I had laid claim to Raisa in the cave, feeding from my ownership of her and drawing strength from my anger. But when I closed my eyes and pictured Raisa's face, I saw her smiling at me. She loved me. Trusted me. "I'm yours, Ailynn. Always." She might be mine, but I was hers, too. There was a difference.

The painful burn became a warm current. "I am not you. I will never be you."

A great roar tore through my ears, and a large, yawning hole opened before my feet. Looking down, I saw Mogra's figure pinned beneath a slab of rock, smaller and frailer than I could ever remember seeing her. She stared up at me, her face young again. There were lines around her mouth and dark smudges beneath her eyes. "Ailynn, help me."

For a moment, my arm extended. Part of me wanted to free her. She was still my mother. She had loved me once, in her own way. I reached toward her, but as our hands brushed, I felt the crackling of magic and jerked my arm back.

"Ailynn." I felt her presence inside of me, probing at my mind, trying to twist my will. The current between us sparked, leaving me with a piercing headache. I stumbled backwards. The more distance I could put between us, the safer I would be. "Come back," she shrieked. The image of the twisted old hag flashed before my eyes once again. "You are my daughter, you belong to me."

My eyes stung with tears, but not from the pain throbbing in my skull. My mother was truly lost. Only Mogra the Witch was left. It was not the first time I had realized this, but the full truth of it crashed down around me all at once. "You are not a mother to me anymore."

Mogra let out a shriek. Red and white streaks of agony gouged across my mind, a hissing, glowing poker behind my eyes. I screamed, falling to my knees and cradling my face in my hands. I heard a voice mumbling and realized it was mine, "No. Maker, please let it stop. No, please." My stomach heaved, threatening to empty itself on the ground.

"Let. Me. In." The words pounded against my skull like a heavy fist

on a door.

I clapped my hands over my ears. "No. Secutem!" The shield-mark raked my throat, but I spat it out from between clenched teeth. Fire spilled from my fingertips, swallowing the grass at my feet and stretching up endlessly into the air. The shield burned white hot against the black sky until I could see nothing else. The pain receded, and Mogra howled. The earth around me shook and split beyond the border of my shield, but my fire never wavered. I could feel Mogra prowling at its edge, trying to bend its surface, but she could not get through.

At last, the whipping winds faded and the ground beneath my feet stopped trembling. Everything went quiet. I sank to the ground, crying so heavily the tears blinded me, hissing against my cheeks as my fire turned them to steam. I was alone again. The foreign presence in my mind had vanished.

CHAPTER EIGHT

I REGAINED CONSCIOUSNESS SLOWLY. My head throbbed, and I gritted my teeth against the ache. It took me several moments to blink past the blur of color swimming in front of my eyes. Once I did, I caught a flash of gold against the pale brown dust. Raisa lay on her side, still and unmoving, her long hair spilling out across the ground. I crawled over to her as fast as I could.

"Raisa, open your eyes, *Tuathe*. Please." I whispered the word over and over again—*please, please, please*—until I lost it somewhere inside of my mouth and forgot what it meant.

Raisa cried out at the sound of my voice, but her eyes remained shut. I put my hand to her belly, trying to feel the unborn child within her. Raisa's abdomen moved, but not with the light, twitching bumps of quickening. A long, shuddering pull came from somewhere deep inside of her, and fear gouged at my chest.

"Oh no. No, no, no. It's too soon." I scrambled to my feet, running to find my abandoned traveling pack. There was a large tear in the side, but it did not appear to be in bad condition. I ripped open the largest pocket and dug through the supplies, tossing out food and clothing. I clutched the jars and pouches against my chest.

As I turned back, I noticed the change in the landscape for the first time. Instead of a giant pit of mud and stone, a huge, glittering lake stretched out as far as I could see. It was the same shade of blue as the magical scarf. Mogra was nowhere to be seen, and I hoped the avalanche had crushed her. I tightened my grip on the small jars and knelt at Raisa's side again. She seemed to sense my shadow over her, because her eyes twitched behind their closed lids.

"It's all right," I doubted she could hear me. "I promise, everything is going to be all right."

"Is she alive?" Hossa asked in a hoarse voice. He appeared behind me, covered in dirt.

"For now, but I need water. Go."

Hossa bowed his head and hurried off toward the lake without another word, but I feared it would make no difference. Raisa's breathing was too fast and shallow, and she tensed with pain even while unconscious. I had seen gravely injured people before, and I had even watched a few die under my mother's care, but nothing had prepared me for seeing Raisa in the same position. I could not lose her. Not after everything we had been through. I forced the fear down, but my hands shook as I reached for one of the jars.

First, valerian root to put you to sleep. I painted several drops over her parted lips and coaxed the rest down her throat. After several long moments, her breathing evened out. I allowed myself to breathe again as well. I rested my hands back over her stomach. Another contraction rippled under my palms, and her face pulled tight, her closed eyes twitching beneath their lids.

Next, belladonna, to take away your pain. I measured the dose carefully. Too little, and it would stimulate her instead of relaxing her. Too much, and she would never wake. I made her swallow the extract as best I could, and the tense line of her body went limp. Her face began to soften, and her muscle spasms weakened. I held my hand in front of her mouth, but I could feel only the faintest wisp of air.

*And then...*I looked down at the remaining jars before me. I could not use aconite or any of the strongest poisons without harming the child. Our child. In a flash, my eyes settled on the small pouch of crampbark I had stuffed in with the rest of the herbs. I rushed to open it. The valerian root and belladonna had already started their work, and Raisa did not resist as I sprinkled it onto her tongue. Hassa arrived moments later with a full skein of water. I snatched it from his hands and tipped it against her mouth.

"Drink," I urged. It took some effort, but I got her to swallow. This time, I did not feel anything when I rested my palm over her abdomen.

"How is she?" Hassa asked.

I shrugged. "I don't know. I don't think she's going to deliver prematurely, but I had to give her some very powerful herbs. They might do more harm than good if I measured wrong."

"You saved us from Mogra, young witch." Hassa placed his large hand on my shoulder. "I think that you will save them, too."

"We can't move them." I was too overwhelmed to respond to his hopeful words. "But I know this is a bad place to stay, and we have no idea what happened to Mogra."

Hassa shook his head. "She will not come after us now. If she is still alive, she will wait. You surprised her today, and she will need more time to gather her forces."

I nodded. As twisted as she had become, Mogra had not lost all of her cleverness. Waiting before she planned another strike sounded exactly like her. Still, I could not banish all of my fear. "And if she does come?"

"Then we will be ready for her."

* * *

I spent the next several hours watching Raisa. Her condition remained mostly unchanged, but it did not worsen either, which was a good sign. I stroked her hair, careful not to irritate the puffy line of a cut across the back of her head. All of us were covered in bruises and scrapes thanks to the avalanche. I had taken some of the leftover belladonna extract to ease the ache in my joints, and one of Hassa's arms was draped in a loose binding to cover a nasty gash beneath his shoulder. Still, he remained watchful as he circled our little camp, gazing out over the smooth blue surface of the lake.

"Perhaps you should sleep," he said after a while. "You look almost as exhausted as she does."

I shook my head. I had already abandoned Raisa when she needed me once before. I would not do so again, no matter what happened. "I'll sleep later. I need to make sure she remains stable through the night. She's barely at sixteen weeks. The baby can't come now." I left the rest of the thought unspoken. They would not survive.

Hassa looked at me. "Sixteen weeks? I thought that your kind carried for nine months. How is she so large already? Or do humani always look like that?"

I had my suspicions about that. Since Raisa was stable for the moment, I decided to give her another examination. "I think she is carrying twins," I said as I ran my hands over her stomach. It was far more pronounced now than it had been even a few days ago. "It is unusually early to feel quickening, especially with a first pregnancy and she is very large." Using my fingers, I tried to confirm the position of one of the tiny bodies. "Yes, I think there are two."

Twins. Even more joy, or even more pain. Raisa shifted beneath me, trying to become more comfortable. The sedatives and muscle relaxants were working. I put the soft part of my traveling pack beneath her head, trying to make her more comfortable. I had done everything I could for her, and only time would show how well she would recover.

"What are you going to tell her when she wakes up?" Hassa asked.

"That I love her," I whispered. I cupped the side of her face, stroking my thumb over the point of her cheek. Her breath came out in a long sigh, but she did not wake up. "That even though I know this is frightening, she doesn't have to do it alone. I'll be there to help her this time."

Hassa gave me a long look, and I thought I saw him bow his head before he headed back toward the lake, offering me a little more privacy. I stretched out on the ground beside Raisa, resting my head near her shoulder and folding a gentle arm around her waist. "I love your mother very much, you know," I said as I stroked my hand over the swell of her belly. Small twitches and bumps underneath my hand reassured me that, for now, the children were still moving. It almost felt like they were listening to me, responding to my voice. I convinced myself that if the babies were still alive and well, Raisa would be, too.

My chest was sore and tight with the tears I had been too terrified to shed, and they broke in my voice. "You were not conceived in joy, but I promise that you will be born into it. I will give you my protection and of my knowledge. You will be my princes. I will give you anything you want." The words sent gooseflesh crawling over my skin. They sounded too much like Mogra, and I wanted to take them back. "But most of all, I promise to love you. I will not be like my mother."

A few moments later, Raisa's eyes fluttered open. Her right hand reached for mine, holding it tight against her stomach. She shivered as the babies stirred inside of her, and her soft smile faltered. "Is he all right? Please, Ailynn, tell me that he's all right."

"They," I corrected her, lacing my fingers with hers. I could not keep the truth from her now that I knew. "They are both alive."

"Two?" Although Raisa's eyes were still clouded with pain and weariness, they widened.

I released her hand and rubbed her forehead, smoothing away the worry lines and checking to make sure that her skin did not feel warm. "Two," I repeated. "We have two children. That is why you are growing so quickly."

For a moment, Raisa looked frightened, as though she was wondering how she could possibly handle two children at once, but her eyes locked with mine and I felt her draw her reassurance from me. It felt wonderful to be there for her this time, especially since I had not been able to offer her strength or comfort before. The scars of guilt inside of me began to fade.

"Two," she sighed, leaning back against my shoulder. "Then we are doubly blessed."

I smiled. It had taken a while, but I was beginning to view them as a blessing instead of a burden as well. "I love you," My fingertips drifted over her lips so that she could kiss them. Her eyes closed and the corners of her mouth turned up in a small smile despite the pain. "And I love them. Now, sleep."

Raisa obeyed and closed her eyes. I sighed and sat back on my heels, observing her as best I could in the dark. Our children had settled back down, and I felt no more movement under my hand. I suspected they were following their mother's example and resting for a while.

Our children.

My chest locked up, cutting off my breath as the thought echoed in my head. I remembered thinking the same thing while Raisa had hovered on the edge of death. *Ours.* Only now, when I had nearly lost the most important people in my life, did I understand just how much they meant to me. "My sons," I said, mouthing the words in quiet disbelief.

"And how do you know they will be sons?" Raisa murmured quietly in the darkness. "Do you have the sight now as well, *Tuathe*?"

"No, I'm only guessing. But I am a witch's daughter." I could say that now without humiliation or shame. My mother was a part of me, and her knowledge had helped me to save Raisa's life, but she did not dictate my actions. She could not control me anymore.

"You're more than that," Raisa said before she drifted back to sleep. "So much more."

I smiled and closed my eyes. With her, I felt as though I could be more.

Rae D. Magdon

CHAPTER NINE

IT TOOK US THREE more days to reach Liarre territory. I insisted on a slower pace than usual, concerned traveling might upset Raisa's recovery, but she had regained most of her strength by the time we reached our destination. The borderline turned out to be a stretch of high brush, a sharp contrast from the bare canyon faces and sharp outcroppings that had surrounded us for the past several weeks. The brush was high enough to reach my upper arms, but Hassa stood well above it, and it only brushed Raisa's ankles as she rode on his back.

"What do you think, Ailynn?" Raisa asked. "Better or worse than a bunch of rocks?"

I frowned, stopping to tug my shirt free of a stray branch. "Worse," I muttered. "At least the rocks don't reach out to grab you."

"Stay close," Hassa said as I hurried to catch up. "Humans are a rare sight here. You would not be welcome without me as your escort."

I walked beside him in silence for the next several minutes, but I began to hear other sounds over my own crunching footsteps. Soft rustling, almost like sighs, drifted over the top of the undergrowth. At first, I thought some small animal must be scurrying for cover, but the noise grew steadily louder. I turned to Hassa for reassurance. "Do you hear that? I think we're being followed."

"So we are," he said, unafraid of whatever was following us. "The Liarre are seen only when we want to be seen, and heard only when we want to be heard. The border guards are letting you know that they are here."

I glanced over my shoulder, squinting as I tried to discern any difference in color or texture that might give one of the hiding Liarre away, but I could not see anything. It was difficult to imagine a creature as large as Hassa hiding himself in the brush, but perhaps some of the other races were more adept at camouflage.

The brush finally faded into knee-high weeds and grass, and we began to climb over a low, rolling slope. "Over the crown of the hill is the valley of Ardu," Hassa said, gesturing with his hand. "The Liarre capital is one of the oldest and most beautiful cities on the continent. It was built long before the Creator made us, but we have modified it for our own use over the centuries."

Even with the warning, the sight that stretched out before me when I reached the top of the hill took my breath away. A wide dirt path led down the side of the hill and into a sharp dip in the landscape. Nestled in the valley was some of the most stunning architecture I had ever seen. Instead of stairways, spiraling ramps surrounded the outer walls of the taller buildings. To our right sat a large, angular structure that reminded me of an hourglass. An ancient-looking stone wall surrounded the entire city, rising and falling with the shape of the earth.

Raisa let out a gasp as well. Her hand reached down to grab my shoulder, and I knew that she wanted to draw what she had just seen. Instead, she stared with wide eyes. "It's beautiful," she murmured. "I've never seen buildings like that, not even in my books. They're so tall." I smiled up at her, and I thought I saw the shimmer of tears in her eyes. This was the first city Raisa had ever seen in person. Mogra had never allowed us to travel far as children, and Raisa had remained trapped in the cave while I travelled the world.

Hassa cleared his throat, drawing me from my thoughts and Raisa from her breathless study of the city. "You will have more chances to see Ardu from a distance. The young mother needs rest and food, and your friends are waiting for you. I am sure that they are anxious to greet you."

Overlooking Raisa's needs made me feel slightly guilty, but I did not worry too much as I gazed at the pleased expression on her face. Some color had already begun to return to her cheeks. "Come on," I said, squeezing her hand. "Let's go see it up close."

The walk down the steep hillside was easier than I expected, but I was surprised when we did not follow the main road. Instead, we traveled down a narrow, winding footpath that took us out of our way several times. Sensing my curiosity, Hassa answered my unspoken question. "These are dangerous times. Many of the main roads have been blocked off or defended with traps."

The closer we got to the city itself, the wider and more well used the path appeared to become. "This place is amazing," Raisa whispered as a large pair of wood and iron gates rose high above us. The wall also grew taller as we drew closer, and I was impressed by how well defended the Liarre were. If the Queen did decide to extend her reach beyond Amendyr, Ardu would not be an easy city to conquer.

My eyes caught a hint of movement on top of the gate, and the pair of doors swung open with a loud, reluctant groan. The three of us walked into the city, past several groups of curious onlookers that watched and whispered in a language I did not understand. Although I had known what to expect after meeting Hassa and Jinale, I was still unnerved by the sight of the Liarre as they gathered around us. Their proportions seemed wrong, and the sight of their claws and teeth made my heart race. They seemed similarly wary of us, and most did not bother to hide their stares.

"You will have to forgive them," Hassa explained. "Some of them have never seen a human before. The Liarre have as many myths and legends about your race as you do about ours."

"What about Cate and Larna? I thought you said they were here?"

"They are Wyr. They might look like you sometimes, but it is not the same. Come, I can show you the place where they are staying."

I caught sight of two small, familiar figures among the crowd, and I grinned. "No need. They're already here."

Raisa looked at me with a silent question as Cate and Larna came into view. I nodded, and she climbed down from Hassa's back. The two women hurried towards us, calling out a greeting. Their movements gave them away, marking them as something more than human. They walked with the rolled, loping gait of wolves even though they were on two legs, and I understood what Hassa had meant when he said they were not the same.

As soon as they reached us, Cate wrapped me in a tight embrace. "Ailynn, thank the Maker you arrived safely. I was worried something had happened to you."

"Several things happened," I admitted. "But at least we're here safe."

Cate's expression could only be described as chastising. "You seem to enjoy rushing into dangerous situations. In fact, I believe that's how we met."

"I do not," I protested. "I wasn't looking for trouble this time. Once I freed Raisa, Mogra followed us. Then, the rest of our party—"

"Is probably fine," Raisa interrupted, sounding more confident than I felt. "Jinale will bring them back safely. Without Mogra behind them, I am sure they escaped the kerak and the shadowkin."

"Good." Cate released me and moved to hug Raisa. "I hope I haven't made you uncomfortable, but I feel as though I already know you. My name is Cate."

Raisa smiled and returned the hug. "It's all right. Ailynn speaks of you often, and I feel as though I know you as well. Besides, I'm in your debt. Without you, Ailynn would be dead and I would still be locked away."

Larna stepped forward and clasped Raisa's hands. She was not as comfortable with touch as her mate, but she was still very friendly. "Cate spent a long time looking for the spell to free you. We are glad to have you here."

The bottom dropped from my stomach. "Oh no, the book," I said, remembering. "I left it behind. I forgot all about it after Mogra summoned the great wind."

"Don't worry," Cate said. "The book doesn't matter, at least not to me. Ellie's wife will be sad to hear that it was lost, but it's only an object. At least you arrived safely, and I'm sure that the others will, too."

"I wouldn't say we arrived safely," I said. "We almost died." The echo of fear welled up inside of me again, and I could not help stealing a glance at Raisa's stomach. Nothing had changed, and I forced the memories down.

Larna followed my gaze and smiled. "I am thinking there is more than one pup in there. Am I right?"

Since she was clearly too polite to ask, Raisa took Larna's hand and placed it over her belly. "Yes. Ailynn says we're having twins." The use of the word 'we' did not disturb me anymore. Instead, I felt a surge of warmth. Cate gave me a small, approving nod. I was not sure how much she knew about the circumstances of Raisa's pregnancy, but surely she did not need her Sight to realize they were not mine. *No, not of my blood, but they are still mine.*

"That is unusual for humans," Larna said. "Have you felt quickening yet?"

"Yes."

Cate sighed and curled a fond arm around Larna's waist. "You act like you've never seen a human pregnancy before, *Tuathe*. Sometimes you forget you were a human for many more years than you have been a Wyr."

Larna removed her hands from Raisa's belly. "I've seen more Wyr give birth than humans. My father made me leave the house when my siblings were born." A shadow crossed her face as she mentioned her family, and the brief look of sadness was poignant enough to make me pull Raisa close against my side.

Cate shuddered. "I like to pretend that Wyr only carry one at a time. The thought of three or four at once is a little overwhelming."

Raisa laughed. "I wasn't even prepared for one, let alone two, and poor Ailynn was just dragged along without anyone asking her opinion."

"I was not," I protested. "And now that we aren't about to die, I'm actually looking forward to it."

"What about Mogra?" Larna asked. "You said she was chasing you. What was her fate?"

I looked over at Raisa, hoping she would take over as resident storyteller for a little while. "We aren't exactly sure," she explained. "Doran gave us three gifts when he left us with the Liarre."

I smiled as she began to tell the story, adding emphasis and embellishments as she went. Raisa had always enjoyed a good tale, and apparently being part of one herself only made the experience of telling it better. Perhaps Cate had Seen some of the tale herself, or maybe Doran had shown her the gifts, because she only asked one question after Raisa finished explaining. "Mogra did not try to cross the lake?"

"No. There was no sign of her after that."

"Not quite," I had not told Raisa about our strange encounter, but I could not resist bringing it up. Perhaps Cate would be able to make some sense of it. "I saw Mogra in my dreams before I regained consciousness. She tried to convince me to help her." I shuddered as I remembered the pain of her consciousness pounding at my head. "Then, she tried to force her way inside of me. It is difficult to describe."

Cate's brow furrowed. "Possession is a form of necromancy. I'm afraid that Mogra is attempting to learn all seven types of magic."

"If she's still alive," Larna added. "The avalanche might have been killing her."

"No," I said. "If she had died, I would know."

Cate gave me a long look, and I sensed the weight of magic behind her gaze. "Be careful, Ailynn. If Mogra is learning necromancy, she is even more dangerous than we thought."

The crowd of curious Liarre had begun to break apart, and I nudged Cate's shoulder. "We'll discuss it more later, but now that the welcoming committee is bored with us, is there somewhere we can clean up and rest? Raisa seems a little pale."

Cate gave me a look. "And you look just as exhausted as she does, Ailynn. Come with us. We'll show you to the guest building, and tomorrow, we will take you to meet Chairwoman Maresth so you can begin your official stay in Ardu." She led us deeper into the city, and I took Raisa's arm, following at her side.

CHAPTER TEN

SENSING OUR NEED FOR privacy, Cate and Larna bid us goodbye as soon as they showed us to our rooms, promising to come by later with food. Although I was sorry to see them go, I was grateful for the chance to rest. Just looking at the large, freshly made bed made my muscles ache a little less. I could hardly remember the last time I had gotten a good night's sleep. Someone had left a clean change of clothes at the foot of the mattress, and I wasted no time stripping off my half-burned shirt, grateful to be free of it at last.

Raisa watched me as I continued undressing, folding her arms across her chest. "It's a nice room. I'm surprised our hosts are so well prepared for human guests. According to the books I've read, the Liarre are very protective of their territory. Most of them consider us a threat."

I shrugged and picked up one of the clean shirts. "They can't be as bad as Mogra and her creatures. Maybe that's why they agreed to let us stay. We have a common enemy."

Before I could pull the shirt over my head, Raisa reached out to stop me. "Let's not talk about Mogra now. She has already consumed your thoughts for the last several weeks." She squeezed my naked shoulder, and I sighed at the gentle touch. "Let yourself relax, Ailynn. Enjoy the fact that we can stop running for a while."

I set the shirt aside, kicking off the rest of my clothes and climbing into the large bed. My jaw stretched in a wide yawn, and I threw my arm over my eyes. "Maybe we should sleep. It's been a while since I slept in a real bed." The mattress dipped as Raisa climbed into bed beside me. I could feel her studying my face. "Come here," I urged, spreading my arms so that she could rest her head on my shoulder. She settled next to me, shifting until she found a comfortable position against my side.

For some reason, sleep would not take me. I opened my eyes again and stared up at the empty ceiling. "I was afraid that you would not come up again from the darkness," I confessed. "I thought I had lost you forever. I would never forgive myself if I failed to protect you again."

Raisa let out a small, frustrated sigh and pulled tighter against me. "Shouldn't I take some responsibility for my own choices? If this past year has taught me anything, it's that love does not make us perfect. You have already forgiven me for my betrayal, but you haven't even begun to forgive yourself. Don't you think you deserve it?"

"But—"

"You did protect me. Look at me." Her fingertips stroked down the curve of my cheek. "Feel me." She leaned forwards until her lips were only a breath away from mine. "I'm here. Right here. And we're safe."

She kissed me. My weariness evaporated.

I undressed her with great care, peeling away her clothes to reveal strips of silken skin. She lifted her arms long enough to help me remove her shirt, wrapping them around me as soon as they were free. My body shivered at the whisper-light caress of her warm hands. Before, we had walked the razor thin wire of need and desperation, the unspoken line of pleasure in possessiveness. This time, we shared slow, trusting kisses, each touch a sweet promise.

"Is this all right?" I asked as I kissed along her collarbone, familiarizing myself with the taste of her skin.

"More than all right." She placed her hand over my rapidly beating heart and smiled when it stuttered out of rhythm. "Does my touch do that to you?" The shaking fingertips of her other hand traced the shape of my face, drawing light patterns over my cheeks and chin. They touched the sensitive edges of my lips, following the curve and dipping just between until I was kissing them.

"You know it does."

Raisa's palms trailed along my shoulders as my hand crept into the stiff confines of her leggings. I only meant to untie the front, but when she pushed forward and swung one of her legs over my waist to straddle me, I pushed further than I intended. My fingertips slid through slick, clinging warmth, and I caught my bottom lip between my teeth to stifle a groan. She gasped at the sudden contact, and the sound coaxed an answering pulse from between my own legs.

"And that is what your touch does to me," she sighed, tipping her head back. "I love you, Ailynn. So much."

For a moment, I was tempted to push forward and slip inside of her, but I drew my hand back instead. I wanted to make love to her properly, without the blinding urgency that had driven us before, not this way, still half-clothed and desperate. Raisa whimpered when I removed my fingers, but allowed me to ease her leggings the rest of the way down her thighs. "Ailynn, I need..." she said in a strangled whisper, unable to complete her thought.

"You need?" I prompted. Hearing that I was loved and wanted was a balm for all of my old hurts.

"I need you. Just you. I always have."

This time, there were no barriers between us as I sank inside of her. She clutched tight around my fingers, hot, slick, and impossibly smooth. Her breath hitched, and the swollen bud of her clit twitched against the heel of my palm. I pressed deeper, and her head tipped back, sending her hair spilling down between her shoulder blades in a winding golden river. I pushed myself up with my free arm, burying my face in the sweet curve of her neck. The shift changed the angle of my fingers, and Raisa clutched the sides of my arms as her inner walls rippled. Her low gasps made my head spin, but I ignored my own need. After all we had been through, she deserved this careful, loving attention.

Raisa began to rock forward, urging me to quicken my pace. She draped her warm, slender leg over mine, sliding her hand down the curve of my side to cup my hip. But it was not enough. I had to feel more of her. I explored her shoulders with my mouth, dipping down to tease the tips of her breasts to hardness. She gasped and shuddered, so responsive under my tongue. I ached to feel more of her. I tipped her backward, slowing my thrusts as I began to kiss my way lower.

I tried my best to pace myself, taking time to learn the curve of her stomach, follow the flair of her hips, stroke the twitching muscles in her thighs with my palms, but she was impatient. She touched my cheek, brushing the curtain of loose hair away from my face to meet my eyes, and I could not resist her while she looked at me with such need.

Stealing one final glance at Raisa's flushed face and kiss-swollen lips, I draped one of her legs over my shoulder and lowered my head. I did not hesitate, pushing forward with an insistent tongue, wrapping my lips around her and sucking hard. The taste, the heat, the soft sounds that spilled from her lips as her head tipped back, shook my soul.

I tried to delay it, to build her up with slow, rhythmic sweeps of my tongue, but Raisa could only hold back for so long. I felt a surge of love and pride as she arched off of the bed. One of her hands fisted the sheets while the other wove into my hair, holding me close as her entire body trembled. Unwilling to stop, I rode the crest of the wave with her. I pushed up, seeking the place inside of her that would send her shattering to pieces. A burst of sweetness hit my lips, and a sob tore in her throat, a broken piece of my name.

The deep, crushing spasms slowly faded to small twitches. Raisa finally let go of my hair and collapsed backwards, the strain in her face softening into a broad smile. I shifted higher to leave another kiss on her stomach, but found myself pulled up to her waiting mouth instead. She caught my lower lip between her teeth, tugging on it lightly before nuzzling just under my chin. Raisa quickly seized control, coaxing my hands to wind through the slats of the headboard.

At last, her teasing touches made their way down to the sensitive line between my hips, tracing back and forth until I was sure I would go mad. I ached for her to move lower, to claim me and offer reassurance and love. My lungs could not seem to take in enough air, and my heart tried to pound its way out of my chest. Every inch of my skin seared with a fierce, burning heat. "Please," I begged, spreading my thighs wider and lifting my hips in invitation. "Touch me."

The first gentle brush of her fingers made my body seize and shiver. A rush of heat escaped, and wetness spilled out to meet her hand. I was a little embarrassed at my lack of control, but Raisa only gazed down at me in wonder. She pushed inside of me with one gliding motion, and the sudden chapfullness stole my breath. I could feel her against me, within me, all around me. Our foreheads met, and her warm breath whispered against my cheek. "Oh, Ailynn. You are so beautiful."

Raisa's hand stroked up and down my side in a soothing line as her fingers began to twist, easing back, and then sinking forward again. I shivered at the stretch, but did not make a sound. The rush of heat between my legs had me blossoming open against her hand, and I felt vulnerable and exposed as she pushed deeper inside of me. "Relax," she murmured. "Let me love you."

I let go and gave myself over to her touch, sighing in relief as the last coils of tension in my muscles loosened their grip. My hips bucked as her thumb began to roll over the sensitive tip of my clit. I allowed myself to sigh, to gasp her name, to rock against her hand, and take the pleasure she offered me. Her fingers found a sensitive place that made me sob, and for a split second, I was certain I would shatter into a thousand pieces.

My peak came as a deep, shuddering thing, sharp and aching of pleasure. I felt myself flooding over, pouring into her, wanting to be as close to her as possible. Each pulse forced tears from my eyes. I clutched at Raisa's shoulders, and her hand tangled in my hair, curving around the back of my neck and guiding our lips together. She kept kissing me as the hand between my legs stilled, unwilling to let me pull away. I had no desire to leave.

"We are finally together, aren't we?" Raisa whispered, and I knew what she meant. We had touched each other in anger, in pain and desperation, but never softly, never slowly, simply because we were two people in love. It was the same, and yet it was wholly different.

"Yes, we are," I said once I had caught my breath. "I love you, Raisa."

"I love you too, *Tuathe*." I sighed, resting my arm over the swell of Raisa's stomach. "They stir when you touch me," she breathed, closing her eyes and kissing my cheek once, twice.

"When I touch your stomach?" I asked sleepily.

"Yes, and sometimes when they hear you talking. They already know you." She paused for a moment, gripping my shoulder a little tighter. "Tell me a story, Ailynn? They aren't the only ones who love the sound of your voice."

I looked down into her soft eyes, but she seemed completely serious. "What? My other services weren't enough to entertain you?"

"That was very entertaining, but we would like a story to fall asleep to."

"We would?" I reached down to rub circles on her abdomen, and felt a flutter of movement against my open palm. The request reminded me of simpler times when I had lulled her to sleep with my voice. The memories were happy instead of bittersweet, and I welcomed them with open arms.

Raisa beamed up at me and curled her hand over mine. "Yes, we would."

"Which story?"

"They haven't heard the story of Princess Kirste and Ara. You know, the one where the King gives his daughter a mermaid as a birthday present."

I dropped a lingering kiss on her forehead. "If you know it so well, perhaps you should tell it. You're a better storyteller than I ever was."

"Hardly, but if you insist, I suppose we can tell it together. You start."

I gave in and pulled Raisa closer against my side. "All right. The sight of the beautiful creature before her sucked Kirste's breath out of her chest. Her light-colored hair was long and swept to one side, and a filmy white sheet was draped over her shoulders..."

The End

About Rae D. Magdon

Rae D. Magdon lives and works in the state of Alaska. Over the past few years, she has written several lesbian-themed novels, including *Dark Horizons, The Second Sister, Wolf's Eyes* and her first published work written with Michelle Magly, *All The Pretty Things*. *Dark Horizons* and *Wolf's Eyes* were finalists in the Science Fiction/Fantasy category for the 2014 Rainbow Awards.

She enjoys writing fantasy and science fiction, in addition to modern-day romances. When she is not writing original fiction, she ~~wastes~~ spends her time dabbling in ~~unapologetically smutty~~ romantic lesbian fanfiction. Her favorite fandoms are Law & Order: SVU and Mass Effect. In her free moments, which are few and far between, she enjoys spending time with Tory, her wonderful spouse, and their two cats.

Connect with Rae online

Website - http://raedmagdon.com/
Facebook - https://www.facebook.com/RaeDMagdon
Tumblr - http://raedmagdon.tumblr.com/
Email - rdmagdon@desertpalmpress.com

Other Books by Rae D. Magdon

Available at Smashwords, CreateSpace, Bella Books, and Amazon

Amendyr Series

The Second Sister
ISBN: 9781311262042

ELEANOR OF SANDLEFORD'S entire world is shaken when her father marries the mysterious, reclusive Lady Kingsclere to gain her noble title. Ripped away from the only home she has ever known, Ellie is forced to live at Baxstresse Manor with her two new stepsisters, Luciana and Belladonna. Luciana is sadistic, but Belladonna is the woman who truly haunts her. When her father dies and her new stepmother goes suddenly mad, Ellie is cheated out of her inheritance and forced to become a servant. With the help of a shy maid, a friendly cook, a talking cat, and her mysterious second stepsister, Ellie must stop Luciana from using an ancient sorcerer's chain to bewitch the handsome Prince Brendan and take over the entire kingdom of Seria.

Wolf's Eyes
ISBN: 9781311755872

CATHELIN RAYBROOK has always been different. She Knows things without being told and Sees things before they happen. When her visions urge her to leave her friends in Seria and return to Amendyr, the magical kingdom of her birth, she travels across the border in search of her grandmother to learn more about her visions. But before she can find her family, she is captured by a witch, rescued by a handsome stranger, and forced to join a strange group of forest-dwellers with even stranger magical abilities. With the help of her new lover, her new family, and her eccentric new teacher, she must learn to gain control of her powers and do some rescuing of her own before they take control of her instead.

Desert Palm Press

Written with Michelle Magly

Dark Horizons
ISBN: 9781310892646

Lieutenant Taylor Morgan has never met an ikthian that wasn't trying to kill her, but when she accidentally takes one of the aliens hostage, she finds herself with an entirely new set of responsibilities. Her captive, Maia Kalanis, is no normal ikthian, and the encroaching Dominion is willing to do just about anything to get her back. Her superiors want to use Maia as a bargaining chip, but the more time Taylor spends alone with her, the more conflicted she becomes. Torn between Maia and her duty to her home-world, Taylor must decide where her loyalties lie.

Cover Design By : Rachel George
www.rachelgeorgeillustration.com

www.desertpalmpress.com

CPSIA information can be obtained at www.ICGtesting.com
Printed in the USA
BVOW11s0757110715

408279BV00026B/296/P